Slow down. Get a grip!

She was trapped inside...and alone. Margot  careened forward with a giddy feeling of fright, her heart beating a staccato rhythm in her chest. Where was Bellamy?

She turned cautiously away from the sound of the voice . . . away from the strange masked man whose midnight serenade sounded beneath her window. She locked and latched the door, then picked up the telephone. It was dead!

Bellamy, please come back! Margot leaned against the locked door and shivered. A moment later, the wind abated and she heard the hideous song again....

"Margot," the madman sang, "Margot, dear Margot has died in her sleep...."

D0728146

Dear Reader,

What better time to snuggle tightly with the one you love than on All Hallows' Eve—when things truly go bump in the night!

Harlequin Intrigue is ringing your doorbell this month with "Trick or Treat," our Halloween quartet—filled with ghastly ghouls and midnight trysts!

Ever since childhood, Laura Pender's favorite writer was Edgar Allan Poe. His chilling story "Masque of the Red Death" inspired this book. To that, Laura added an isolated lighthouse shrouded in eerie mist and an extremely sexy, extremely dangerous reclusive hero—sure to make your pulse race.

Be sure not to miss any of the TRICK OR TREAT quartet this month.

Regards,

Debra Matteucci
Senior Editor & Editorial Coordinator

Music of the Mist

Laura Pender

Harlequin Books

TORONTO • NEW YORK • LONDON
AMSTERDAM • PARIS • SYDNEY • HAMBURG
STOCKHOLM • ATHENS • TOKYO • MILAN
MADRID • WARSAW • BUDAPEST • AUCKLAND

If you purchased this book without a cover you should be aware that this book is stolen property. It was reported as "unsold and destroyed" to the publisher, and neither the author nor the publisher has received any payment for this "stripped book."

ISBN 0-373-22249-1

MUSIC OF THE MIST

Copyright © 1993 by Laura Pender.

All rights reserved. Except for use in any review, the reproduction or utilization of this work in whole or in part in any form by any electronic, mechanical or other means, now known or hereafter invented, including xerography, photocopying and recording, or in any information storage or retrieval system, is forbidden without the written permission of the publisher, Harlequin Enterprises Limited, 225 Duncan Mill Road, Don Mills, Ontario, Canada M3B 3K9.

All characters in this book have no existence outside the imagination of the author and have no relation whatsoever to anyone bearing the same name or names. They are not even distantly inspired by any individual known or unknown to the author, and all incidents are pure invention.

This edition published by arrangement with Harlequin Enterprises B. V.

® and TM are trademarks of the publisher. Trademarks indicated with ® are registered in the United States Patent and Trademark Office, the Canadian Trade Marks Office and in other countries.

Printed in U.S.A.

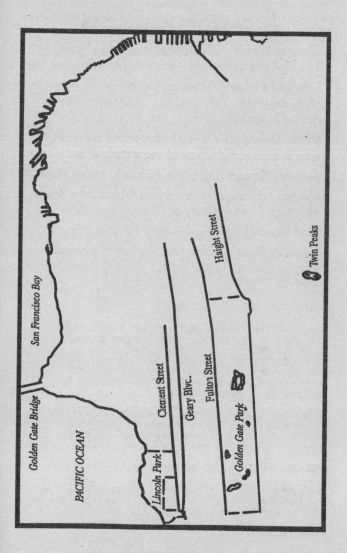

PACIFIC OCEAN

Golden Gate Bridge

San Francisco Bay

Lincoln Park

Clement Street

Geary Blvd.

Fulton Street

Golden Gate Park

Haight Street

Twin Peaks

CAST OF CHARACTERS

Margot Wylde—She feared her appearance in *The Masque of the Red Death* might bring her own.

Edward Bellamy—The reclusive horror writer sent chills down Margot's spine . . . but were they of desire or fear?

Victor Grimaldi—A wild man with the baton, he was in the wrong place at the wrong time.

Jerome Taylor—His absence could haunt them all.

Martin Andrews—A man of a thousand voices . . . Was one of them Margot's?

Neil Roberts—He had a most suspicious past.

Linda Bellisario—She needed her big break—maybe enough to kill for it.

Prologue

Jerome Taylor was no stranger to success. Though his work hadn't attained the mythic status of some writers in his field, his string of popular horror novels had done well enough to provide for some of the better things in life, including the penthouse he occupied in Los Angeles. He was satisfied with his work and his ability to extract a good living from his word processor. As for what he wrote, as long as it continued to come easily, he'd stick with it. He didn't like to work too hard.

Unfortunately, one of his writing projects had gotten him into more work than he had bargained for. At his agent's insistence, he'd taken on the libretto for a modern opera, and while the money was fair enough, it was the lure of having his name on the marquee that had won him over. Now, however, he was dreading the thought of having to go up to San Francisco and hang around while they rehearsed the opera. If he'd given that aspect of the project any thought, he wouldn't have gone through with it.

He'd written one screenplay in his career, and the ordeal of having to be on hand for script changes had convinced him not to write another. He didn't care much for San Francisco, either. It was foggy and damp most nights, and built far too much on the incline. No, he preferred his home to a movie or opera set, and he surely didn't need the aggravation of dealing with people.

Still, he'd written the thing, and now he'd have to see it through.

It was just after dark when he finished packing his suitcase for his trip, and he was dressing for a night on the town when the doorbell rang. Hurriedly buttoning his shirt, he walked to the door and opened it.

"Yes?" he said.

His visitor responded by punching him in the throat, knocking him back into the room with the force of the blow. Before the writer could recover, the intruder had thrown the door shut and grabbed him in a headlock, pushing the startled man across the living room.

Taylor couldn't say anything as the man pushed him toward the glass doors covering the balcony. He was gasping for breath and nearly blinded by pain as he stumbled in his attacker's grip. When he did regain his senses enough to fight back, it was too late.

The man slammed Jerome Taylor's head against the glass of the balcony door, shattering it, then pushed, impaling him on the jagged shards in the frame.

He held him for a moment, taking care to stand clear of the pool of blood that was gathering below the writer's now limp form. Then he stepped back, leaving Taylor hanging on the glass, and kicked a footstool over near the man's splayed feet.

He left the penthouse a moment later, taking the stairs down two floors before getting onto the elevator alone to complete his escape. As he rode the cab to the lobby, he hummed a bit of a song. Then he sang a line of it, contented with the sound of his voice in the small space.

Jerome Taylor would have recognized the words right away if he'd been able to hear them. He'd written them, after all. He would have been surprised that this stranger knew the words to this particular aria, however, for the opera wouldn't premiere until October.

But then, maybe it wouldn't premiere at all.

Chapter One

The fog rolled in from San Francisco Bay shortly after midnight, blanketing the city in a cool shroud of mist that diffused the light of the street lamps to indistinct cones of pearly luminescence and seemed to triple the distance between lamps to further conceal the dangers that might lurk there. Footsteps echoed from nowhere as did the hissing sound of cars passing, and voices drifted in and out of hearing like the words of the dead.

This concealing mist was said to be part of the city's charm, its ambience, but it was also one of its hazards. For in the fog intentions were as blurred as images, and the sound of approaching danger was not always distinctly heard.

Two women walked along a downtown street, moving from one patch of fog to the next and speaking together in low tones. They laughed occasionally as they proceeded, seemingly oblivious to the dangers of the night and the fog. The two, both performers at the San Francisco Modern Opera, had been kept late at rehearsal, just as they'd been late many nights as the opera struggled to put its fall production together.

That struggle was made doubly hard by the recent death of Jerome Taylor, the author of the opera's story and lyrics. This past week, which should have been spent tightening up gaps in the story and honing dialogue with the author, was spent instead in a tiring disarray.

It was their fatigue after another long day that prompted them to walk tonight. They needed to unwind after the stress of rehearsal, letting the cool night air soothe their spirits and ready them for a much-needed rest. Tomorrow would be every bit as difficult as today had been. They could only hope it wouldn't be as long.

Margot Wylde, a mezzo-soprano with the opera, was dressed in a topcoat with a scarf wrapped around her throat, while her companion, an alto named Connie Dwight, was dressed with less care for the climate or her health in an open windbreaker. True to her thoughtful nature, Margot had taken care against the chill night air. The inconvenience of even a slight cold was anathema to a singer, especially a singer playing the lead in an opera, where absolute control of the voice is a must. In deference to her voice, Margot even restrained her conversation to responses while they were outside in the cold.

She was quiet, also, because of a strange feeling of being watched that had come over her since the author's untimely death. She couldn't seem to shake the feeling of somebody's eyes upon her throughout the day. She expected that the feeling was groundless, but still it persisted, and the fog strengthened its hold on her heart.

Margot's long dark hair fluttered fitfully in the errant breezes as they walked. The light of street lamps raised a gentle sheen on the rippling tresses that framed her serious oval face, which was marked by strong cheekbones and full expressive lips below the noble line of her nose. Hers was a face fully capable of being sensuous and flirty or steely with determination by turns, making her a favorite with opera patrons and directors alike. At twenty-nine years old, Margot had played most of the world's major opera houses in some of the medium's most demanding roles and was well on her way to becoming one of the major stars in her art.

Her star was rising on other fronts as well. Before coming to town, she had recorded an album of Cole Porter standards that was released over the summer to rave reviews. As a coloratura mezzo-soprano, Margot was blessed with a voice suitable for many mediums of expression. Capable of many of the virtuoso trills and glissandos of coloratura, her deeper soprano voice wasn't cursed by the tendency to become shrill in the upper register, giving her the control of a soprano with the throaty sensuality of a mezzo. In short, it would take an act of God to stop her from fulfilling a unique and glorious destiny as a singer.

It would take an act of God...or one fog-shrouded act of man. Perhaps that was the reason for her uneasy feeling. Maybe, just because things were going so well, she expected something bad to happen. Her career had progressed so smoothly until now.

As they passed before the closed shops that lined the misty streets of the city, Connie spoke in an animated manner, accenting her sentences with laughter, which seemed always ready to burst forth from her expressive features. A strawberry blonde, she was the perfect counterpart to Margot's darker looks and more somber moods—ever since they'd roomed together in college they had each been yin to the other's yang. In fact, it was Connie who convinced Margot to take a two-year position in the repertory company.

Margo liked the city so much after arriving that she had taken the ultimate step of agreeing to purchase a home of her own in the area. She had learned the value of having a home base and intended the California coast to be hers. But, in a move somewhat contrary to her nature, she'd done more than purchase a house. She'd signed the papers to purchase an old lighthouse just south of the city. It was the first time she'd done anything extravagant with the money she'd earned in five years of singing professionally. And, though it severely depleted her savings, she had managed to pay nearly seventy-five percent of the asking price down—a feat that impressed her realtor immensely.

"It'll be lonely out there," Connie said as they turned the corner toward the apartment they were currently sharing. "And the place is probably haunted."

"I hope so," Margot replied, her full lips twisting into a wry smile.

"Won't you be nervous living alone that far from civilization?"

"I'm only about thirty miles outside the city limits, Connie," Margot said with a laugh. "It's even got electricity. And I probably won't have to put up with crank callers, either."

"Oh, those were a couple of wrong numbers, that's all. Besides, I usually never get any strange phone calls."

"You're just lucky, I guess," Margot said. That fact bothered her, too. The only time the mysterious phone calls, with no greeting, not even breathing on the other end, had come to Connie's number was when Margot was there to receive them.

"Well, I'd hate to live alone down there."

"You sound as though you want me to room with you forever. I appreciate the offer, but I don't think you have the space."

"Heck no," Connie quipped, "I'm planning on coming out to live with you as soon as the paint's dry."

"You're certainly welcome anytime."

"Oh, I know, you'll get to living down there with the other hotshots and you won't have time for us bit players." Connie laughed, the sounds of her mirth fading into the fog around them. "It's the classic story."

"There aren't any hotshots living there, are there? I hadn't really checked out the neighborhood very well, but I don't remember there being more than one other house nearby."

"You don't know about your neighbor yet?"

"That big house north of mine?" she asked. It felt strange to use the possessive form in reference to real estate. Strange, but good.

"Sure. That's Edward Bellamy's house," Connie replied, speaking as though she expected Margot to recognize the name.

"And he is?"

"Oh, I forgot, you're all work and no play, aren't you?" Connie laughed again. "Well, if you'd been anywhere near a bookstore lately, you'd know who he is. Far be it from me to attempt to educate you now. He's a friend of Victor's though." Victor Grimaldi was the company's musical director and the author of the music for *The Masque of the Red Death,* the opera that they were rehearsing.

"So he's a writer?" Margot taunted her friend, smiling, though she did seem to recall the man's name now that her memory had been jogged.

"Oh, you!" Connie laughed happily, content to have her friend back again to enjoy their easy conversations and banter. "There was talk that he was supposed to write the script for *Masque,* but the opera board wouldn't pay him enough. That's why they hired Jerome Taylor."

"The poor man," Margot said. "When I think of tripping and falling through a glass door like that, I can't help but cringe."

"Some people have suggested that he committed suicide rather than come up here to face us," Connie said.

"That's terrible!"

"Maybe, but you can't tell me that you're not gagging over his lyrics. Taylor wasn't cheap, either. If they'd hired Edward Bellamy, they would at least have gotten something for their money."

"Taylor is dead," Margot said. "Let it go at that."

"It's probably for the best, anyway. If he'd showed up here, Daniel Pressman probably would have killed him. You know, he probably did it anyway just to sell tickets."

"Let's not talk about it out here. The fog gives me the creeps," Margot said, stopping abruptly and listening. "Wait. Did you hear that?"

"What?"

"Someone singing," Margot said. "It sounded like a bit from the opera."

"Couldn't be."

"Not unless someone else in the cast lives near here. Probably just the wind," Margot said, resuming her measured stride toward the apartment.

"Or you're spooked by our little Halloween opera," Connie suggested. "Come on, let's get some hot chocolate."

The women continued along the empty street toward the apartment they had shared since Margot's arrival last June.

Only the fog knew of their danger, the fog and the man who followed at a discreet distance. Concealed in a trench coat and muffler much like Margot's attire, his face covered by the shadow beneath the lowered brim of his gray fedora, he stopped trailing them when they reached the building. He watched their indistinct forms climb the steps and go into the building, then he turned away, humming softly to himself. He paused after a few steps and let his voice open up into a bit of song.

His was a clear, controlled tenor, but he let it move up as he sang, slipping into a falsetto that was nearly as strong and pure as a woman's voice but lacking the piercing quality that often mars such singing. After a single phrase, he stopped and laughed quietly. Then he continued walking away from the building, his dark form disappearing into the mist.

The fog remained, as discreet about his presence as it is about any of the dangers shrouded within it. Cool and secretive, the fog concealed all crimes.

THE LIGHTHOUSE had been out of service for five years and had stood empty for three of those years after the lightkeeper moved away. Largely through governmental inertia rather than any largess on its part, the Department of the Interior had allowed him to live there after the light station was officially deemed obsolete. Inertia had similarly kept the government from putting the light station up for sale, along with its ten acres of rolling meadowland atop the cliffs south of the city, even after the property was vacant.

All of which worked in Margot's favor, as it had timed her decision to seek local housing for the second week the property was listed. Even so, she might have missed the chance to live in majestic seclusion atop the cliffs overlooking the sea if Victor Grimaldi hadn't mentioned that the lighthouse was available. Her realtor took Margot out eagerly, using the rather lengthy drive to recite the benefits of life outside of the city and discounting the distance as being "well within range of anything you might wish for in the city."

In the end it was the lighthouse itself that sold Margot, making her overcome her prudent nature to take a step much larger than she'd contemplated. The white stucco structure stood proud and tall several hundred feet above the rocky shore at the base of the cliff, its attendant light-keeper's home, covered by weathered shake siding, attached to its base like the foot of an L pointing north along the cliff face. The two-story house itself was roomy, especially for a single woman, and a plenitude of windows let the light into every room at all times of day. The upper level looked as if it hadn't been used for anything recently, although the two large rooms could easily be converted to a suite of rooms for her bedroom and a music room. There was other work to be done to make the building suit her tastes, but it had seemed like home when she walked into it. She felt she belonged there.

Besides, the length of her commute to the city was of little consequence, since she would only be with the company for two years. After that, she would be back to her nomadic routine. But this time, her life would be marked by the existence of this one point of solidity, with the noble tower serving as her personal beacon to guide her home.

AFTER ANOTHER WEEK of grueling rehearsals on the opera's production of *The Masque of the Red Death,* a play loosely based on the Edgar Allan Poe short story of the same name, Margot neared her new home for her first night of residency. She felt a knot of excitement in her throat as she drove her car along the twisting road that skirted the top of the cliff going south from the city. The woman whose main possessions two weeks ago were pri-

marily a large assortment of constantly packed luggage
was now a homeowner.

She was also learning of the many pitfalls involved in
home ownership. The charming house that had made her
feel so welcome had needed extensive work on its plumb-
ing and wiring, a fact that delayed her occupancy for days
while she paid overtime to speed the completion. Now,
having updated the necessary fixtures, she was having the
house remodeled by another crew of young men who
seemed to have all the time in the world to complete their
task.

She would be living in the shambles of a home for a
week or two yet, but she couldn't wait any longer. Disre-
garding her instinct to avoid contaminating her throat
with the dust of the work in progress, she had stored most
of her things in the large circular room at the base of her
lighthouse and moved into what would be a guest room
when the work was completed. She just couldn't stay away
from her new home.

Her home!

The newness of that phrase still pleased her as she drove
through the early night beneath the canopy of stars that
seemed to have brightened especially for her drive.

One thing she had already resolved was that no matter
how much pressure might come from future develop-
ment, she would keep her acreage intact, maintaining a
buffer of open land between herself and any new housing
that might come into the area. She wasn't afraid of sub-
urban sprawl encroaching too badly, however. The landscape wouldn't allow much of it. There were only a couple
miles between her cliff and another rocky slope of moun-
tain to the east, and a large part of the land to the north
was already owned by the writer Connie had mentioned a
week before. To the south was a wildlife preserve. She was

at the end of the lonely road from the city, and it looked as though she would stay that way.

As she rounded the last curve before her house, Margot was surprised to see lights on in Edward Bellamy's home. The two-story Neo-French house was spilling a spear of light across the yard from the tall, arched window of the north, seaside room. Two rooms, actually. It was designed as a passive solar home, and Margot could see how the tall window began in the first-floor room and continued to the room above it. With the lights in both rooms on and the curtains open, the design gave it the look of a vast architectural model rather than an inhabited house. The house contained a large amount of glass, too much for Margot's tastes, yet had retained a look of aloof grandeur every time she had passed it on her nearly daily journeys to check the progress of work on her own home. Signs of habitation took some of that detached quality away, however, making it seem more welcoming.

Since Mr. Bellamy was finally home, Margot decided that it was as good a time as any to say hello to her new neighbor. Or, more properly, *she* was the new neighbor, wasn't she? All the more reason to stop in briefly as soon as possible. As it was only nine o'clock and he was obviously awake, she decided to stop even before going home. Once she was in her house, she didn't want to leave for the night.

She drove in past the twin brick gateposts marking the end of Bellamy's driveway and along the slow curve of asphalt that skirted the front of the house and ended in a double garage designed to match the house in every detail including the arched windows. Parking her car before the black door set in the face of the redbrick house, Margot got out and stretched a bit to loosen the kinks from the drive. Then she walked up to the door and

pressed the button beneath the speaker grill of an intercom system.

"Yes?" a husky baritone replied. His tone wasn't par-
ticularly inviting, and Margot worried for a moment that
she was interrupting him at his work.

"Hi, I'm your new neighbor," she said, leaning toward the speaker. "I just wanted to introduce myself."

"Okay," he answered. "Come on in."

The door before her clicked, unlocking itself for her
entry. Margot turned the knob, feeling somewhat like the
heroine in a horror movie opening the door that everyone in the audience is screaming for her to leave alone.

The entryway was sparsely decorated with an oak table
and chair standing on a flagstone floor. A small Oriental
rug filled the center of the space between the door and the
arched entry to the hall. The front door clicked behind
her, causing her to jump slightly as it locked itself.

"Straight in and to the right," the voice said to her
from a hidden intercom speaker. "I'll be down in a sec."

Margot followed his directions, walking along a short,
dark hall. Despite his seeming extravagance in lighting the
house when seen from outside, Edward Bellamy clearly
wasn't one to waste electricity.

The room she entered was large and comfortable. Two
tall windows filled the adjoining walls to the north and
west. A large desk occupied the corner between the windows, a computer on it alive with the undulating pattern
of a screen-saving program, and a pair of comfortably
padded jade green love seats formed a V about four feet
in from the wall on the inside corner of the room. A reclining chair in a print matching the couches was placed
so that the person seated in it could look out of the window at the sea. The room was large enough so that the

pool table didn't crowd it, but not so large as to lose the informal feeling of the space.

It was well decorated, but clearly to a man's liking, with dark colors predominating. Bookcases with glass doors to shield the volumes inside covered the remaining walls. The top of one low bookcase was decorated with sturdy knickknacks. A small ceramic bust of Edgar Allan Poe stood aloof among them, reminding Margot of Bellamy's supposed connection to the opera.

She walked over to the small bust and studied it absently, finding that what she'd taken for artwork was in fact an award. *Sea of Storms:* Best Novel, read a plaque on the base of the statue.

So he was considered by his peers to be a good writer, anyway, a hopeful sign if he was truly working on the opera.

On the wall above the case, several book covers were framed in dark oak. The cover to *Sea of Storms* was there, as were covers to novels entitled *Storm Garden, Evil Made Easy* and *Whiteout,* among others. Reading the backs of the framed dust jackets, she discovered that Edward Bellamy was a horror writer—a fact that no one had deemed fit to tell her earlier.

But then she hadn't asked, either. Typically wrapped up in her own work, Margot had forgotten her neighbor except when her view of his house brought him to mind. And, among the cast of the opera, it was considered bad form to discuss the work's obvious need of revisions while at rehearsal, except to wonder if it was true that Edward Bellamy would rescue them from a bad libretto now that the original author was beyond helping them.

She turned, looking over the rest of the room for a clue about the house's occupant. A voracious reader as well as a writer, and a pool player. She knew that much. He pre-

ferred dark tones—greens and deep blues—and he liked
to look over the ocean from his reading chair. She noted
from the absence of ashtrays that he didn't smoke, a positive sign.

What else? If the house itself was any indication, he was
ecologically minded. The tall windows continued from
one floor to the next because the floor was open between
levels to allow air flow, not because it created a more
monumental-looking edifice from outside.

"Good evening," announced the same baritone voice
that had greeted her at the door. Without the interference
of the intercom, it was an even deeper, more imposing
sound, and when she turned, she noted that the man
matched his voice.

"Hello," she replied, extending her hand as she walked
toward him. "I'm Margot Wylde, your new neighbor."

"Edward Bellamy." He took her hand in his, engulf-
ing hers completely. "I'm very pleased to meet you."

The man was an inch or two over six feet tall, with a
tanned face that was nearly square. His jaw cleaved
slightly beneath full wide lips that had parted in a smile,
showing even teeth that seemed unusually white against
his tanned features. His nose was long and straight, but
with a slight ridge just below the thick black eyebrows that
were arched over a pair of eyes so blue that she might have
described them as lapis lazuli. His hair was nearly black,
and he wore it long and swept back from his clear forehead. It fell a couple of inches past the collar of his denim
shirt like the mane of a lion.

Her attention was so taken up by his eyes for a moment that she wasn't prepared to speak, though he was
clearly waiting for her to continue the conversation. "I
hope I'm not too late stopping by," she said haltingly.

"Not at all. I work at night, so I am usually up far later than this." He released her hand, staring at her for a moment as he continued to smile warmly. "I wondered when they would get around to selling the lighthouse property. I had thought about putting in an offer myself. Now, I'm glad that I didn't have the opportunity."

"I am, too. As soon as I saw it, I fell in love with it. It's really quite homey."

"It has a lonely look to it," he commented. "But I suspect that will change now. Houses tend to take on the personality of their owners."

"Is that the case with your home?"

"Yes. Nouveau tomb," he said easily, his eyes focused on hers with laser intensity.

"Have you lived here long?" she asked, trying to ignore the scrutiny of his extraordinary eyes. "I was wondering about the weather."

"I've been here for nearly five years. We're high enough so that any wave action in storms doesn't affect us. I've never noticed the weather to be especially bad." He spread his hands slightly, expansively, saying, "Of course, it can get damn foggy. Would you like something? Coffee, a soda? Maybe you want something stronger to unwind after a long day?"

"I didn't come to impose."

"I know that." He laughed, saying, "Though an unannounced visit is, by definition, an imposition. In any case, a good host provides good hospitality—especially to a neighbor."

"I am imposing," she said quickly. She wasn't sure how to interpret his words, or the smile that went with them. This man had a way of keeping her off-balance.

"No, I'm sorry." He touched her shoulder, his broad hand dancing in and away lightly. "I talk too freely. You aren't bothering me in the least. It may be sexist to say, but I have never found a visit by a woman to be an imposition. Most men, however, are a nuisance beyond belief."

"If it's true, then it's probably not sexist."

"Good. So... you'd probably like a diet-something."

"Any cola would do. Why would you assume I'd want a diet soda? Because I'm a woman?"

"No, because you're an opera singer." He walked to the end of one of the bookcases, where he knelt and opened the last glass door to reveal a small refrigerator. "The last thing you would want is to be called the 'fat lady who sings.'"

Margot laughed, seeing his point. "No, I wouldn't want that."

He brought two cans of cola from the fridge, holding both in one hand while he opened them.

"How did you know my occupation?"

"You're famous," he said. "Of course I know you. But, beyond your occupation and name, I'm at a loss. Why did you choose to live such an ungodly distance from the theater? I'd have imagined an uptown address for someone of your resources."

"I have a short contract with the opera. After that, it will be a long commute no matter where I live. I decided that I'd better grab it now before someone else signed the papers. Actually, it was a friend of yours, I believe—Victor Grimaldi—who told me about the lighthouse."

"Victor? Oh, of course," he said, smiling. "You've been working as a guest soloist, or whatever they might call a voice for hire, until now. Right?" He sipped his soda and waved toward the two love seats by way of inviting her to be seated.

"Yes, a voice for hire," she admitted. She sat on one of the love seats as he took a place on the other.

"And you've done well at it. I mean, your property wasn't cheap, so you must be able to earn more than a living by your voice. I've heard you on the radio lately, too. You should always sing jazz."

"Why?"

"Because you do it beautifully," he said. "Besides, nobody listens to opera." He turned on the couch just then, looking out of the broad window facing the sea.

"Well, I listen to opera," she said quickly. "And I don't sing for the money, or the recognition. Do you write for it?"

"No," he said, looking back toward her. "I know what you mean. Money is unfairly the measure of all work in this country. People have a hard time believing that a writer has any motive besides riches for what he does, and I suspect that the same thing goes for opera singers. Nobody takes into account the number of unpublished authors who keep turning out page after page without a cent to show for it. Or, for that matter, the number of sopranos who spend their careers contentedly in the chorus."

He looked back at the window again, staring through the glass.

"What are you looking at?"

"I thought I saw something outside," he said. "Just a flash of movement. Did you see something?"

"No. Might have been kids, though," she suggested. "They're always up to something."

"There are no kids out here." He turned back toward her, focusing his arresting eyes on her face once more. "There's nobody out here but you and me, Margot."

"Oh." Margot felt flustered by his gaze, as though his eyes were consuming her.

"Do you mind if I call you Margot?" he asked. "Since we're going to be neighbors, after all."

"No, not at all. And you are Edward, right?"

"Yes. I've never been partial to that name, but it does sound good when you say it. Most friends call me Bellamy, though some call me worse."

"I like Bellamy," she said softly, then cleared her throat. "Why did you move out here? Seclusion?"

"I like the view," he said simply.

"You write horror fiction, I see."

"Yes, I like that, too." He smiled and drank, seeming to have run out of words.

"But you don't like opera, I take it."

"Not so far." He shrugged. "Why do you ask?"

"I had heard that you were going to be working on our current production. Is it true?"

"Your current disaster, you mean." He managed to combine a laugh with a sigh to punctuate his sentence. "Yes, I'm the fool they've hired now that the idiot responsible for it is beyond justice."

"Disaster? Is it that bad?"

"Worse. My God, you'd think someone trying to mount an original piece of theater would make an attempt at finding a good author to write it. I mean, even opera needs decent dialogue."

"*Even* opera?" Margot couldn't help the jolt of indignation that rose within her at his words. "What do you mean?"

"Face it, you have to have a good story to have a good show. That's the bottom line. Your producers failed to heed that one rule and now they're halfway through a production of a play that has no plot. No spark of imagination. I wouldn't give two cents for 'high-concept' junk you can describe in one sentence. And though opera may be high concept, it should try not to sound like it."

"Do you ever go to the opera?"

"Not in years. They're too long. Too soporific." He stood then and walked to the window. "Sorry, I'm distracted here. Excuse me a moment, won't you?"

"What is it?"

"I heard something." He smiled wryly, shaking his head. "It almost sounded like someone singing outside. I'll be right back."

Margot sat frozen after he left the room. *Singing?* She herself had heard the phantom singing twice more since hearing it in the fog that night with Connie. The thought that the mysterious song might have followed her was chilling.

A minute later, the author returned carrying something in one hand.

"Someone is getting the jump on Halloween," he said as he crossed to the couch. He was holding a plastic mask in his hand. It was a cheap dime-store devil's mask, complete with horns and goatee, and it grinned up at her now in red-faced malevolence.

"What's wrong?" he asked. "You look as though you've never seen a Halloween mask before."

"Do I?" Margot forced a smile to her lips as she clasped both hands to quell their shaking. "Where did you find that?"

"Lying on the patio." He put the mask aside on the table. "You were probably right about kids. I suppose someone out there had a radio, and that's why I thought I heard singing."

"Of course. So, uh, if you hate opera so much, why did you agree to write one?" she asked.

"Victor asked me to," he said simply. "And I wanted to take a shot at it."

"I heard you were supposed to do it to begin with."

"Yes, Victor had wanted me to write it. The management had other ideas, however." He laughed. "They could have spent their money better by hiring someone who could get the job done at the start rather than shopping in the bargain basement. Now they're paying for it."

"And now that they have decided to pay, you believe you can get the job done?"

"Yes. If I'm going to put my reputation on the line, I'd better believe that I can do it."

"Your reputation? But you write horror fiction."

"You needn't make it sound like a crime." He laughed, obviously used to that tone in people's voices.

"No, I'm sure you're quite good at it, but it's not exactly Hemingway. Crazed maniacs in hockey masks and guys with switchblades for fingers are a bit below standard, even for opera."

"You've seen too many movies," he retorted evenly. "All I meant was that the plot of an opera is mainly a vehicle for the music. It's thin at best. Face it, you don't have much time for plot once you've gotten around the arias and stuff."

"But those 'arias and stuff' are art. Horror is . . . well, I don't know. But it's not art."

"You should try reading horror fiction before you denigrate it."

"I don't see any point in that."

"No, but since you're ripping off Edgar Allan Poe, you might try some of his stuff. Not *Masque of the Red Death,* though, because it's very boring. Or read Bram Stoker's *Dracula* and you might find that opera and horror have a great deal in common."

"Heaven forbid," she said, standing. "Well, I'd better be going. It's been a very interesting conversation, Mr. Bellamy."

"Just Bellamy. You don't have to go." He stood, too, concern tightening his features.

"Yes, I do. It's late." She put her can on the coffee table and began walking toward the door. "I have to be up early to work on our *disaster*. I can show myself out."

"Thank you for coming," he said, grasping her hand. "Feel free to come back any time." He bowed then, kissing her hand and rising with a smile. "It could never be an imposition for you to visit my home."

"Thank you, I . . ." She pulled back slightly, but didn't take her hand away from his. She couldn't remove it any more than she could take her eyes from his or turn away from him as he suddenly stepped closer, lifted his other hand to her shoulder and moved his face closer to hers.

Their lips met briefly, just a friendly brushing of their lips, but that touch carried an electricity beyond mere friendliness. Then he released her, leaving her staring at his suddenly clouded gaze.

"We may be on a first-name basis," she said, finding her voice and propriety in the same instant, "but I don't think we're that friendly, Mr. Bellamy."

"No," he admitted, chagrined. "I, uh, I just never kissed an opera singer before."

"You probably won't ever again, either. Good night, Mr. Bellamy."

She walked out of the room, leaving him standing with his mouth slightly open. A moment later, he heard the front door slam, confirming his suspicion that he'd thrown away his first impression entirely.

What on earth is wrong with you, Bellamy? A beautiful woman walks into your home and you just up and kiss her. Way to go.

And she was beautiful. Probably the most beautiful woman he'd ever—no, he would have to admit that there were women more beautiful. His wife had certainly been among them. But this woman was the most beautiful he could currently imagine.

In her absence, the image of her face lingered like the light of the sun burns into the retina after one stares into its disk. He couldn't remember another woman's looks. And her spirit matched her beautiful face.

She was a woman of wit and poise, an aristocrat of women, and he had offended her. It wasn't just the kiss, either. His babbling about opera had hardly been tactful. He had callously thrown his thoughts out without pausing to listen to them himself.

He would clearly have to get used to dealing with women again. It had been too long. He was too used to the luxury of revising until his words were perfect; he'd forgotten how imperfect he could be in person.

Right now he dearly wished that he could tear the last page out and write it over again.

But in life, there were no revisions.

Chapter Two

Margot was much more sanguine about her neighbor the next morning. She felt quite charitable, in fact, with the sight of the Pacific Ocean two hundred feet below her cliff stretching to infinity, and the memory of his too-blue eyes lingering in her mind. Not everybody liked opera, or should. Still, she found herself wishing that he did.

The sun was burning off the morning mists when she rose and took stock of her surroundings. Her new home. The view inside wasn't as inspiring as the one outside. The living room was a shambles of exposed wall studs, stacked Sheetrock and various carpentry tools left lying to await their owners' return to work today. Though her contractor had assured her that the work would be finished "in no time at all," she wasn't so certain. How could they organize this mess into an habitable abode in less than a month?

The first of the workmen, a dark-haired youth named Tom Gleason, arrived shortly after seven. His punctuality impressed Margot, giving her hope for the rest of the project, and she invited him in for a cup of coffee to start the day.

Music of the Mist

"Looks like hell, don't it?" He sipped at his coffee as he peered around the room. "Don't worry, the last of the job is the messiest. Lots of crap to haul away."

"How long do you think it will take to finish?"

"A week, tops." He nodded, convinced of his appraisal.

"How can you be certain?"

"Because we have to start a new job in a week," he said with a sharp laugh. "Gotta pay a penalty if we're not there on time."

"That's hard to believe. I mean, this room, the bathroom, the solarium are all still torn apart. The kitchen is really nothing but a hot plate at the moment, and my bedroom still has no windows. How can you get all of this together in a week?"

"Putting together is the easy part of a remodeling job," the man said. "It's the tearing out that's hard. You've got to be careful removing the old stuff so you don't wreck anything that you want to keep. We can have these rooms rocked in a day. Taped and primed in two more."

"Rocked?" She was always amazed at the plethora of specialized terms used by various professions, designed, she was sure, to maintain a distance between themselves and those outside the field.

"Sheetrocked. That goes fast. It's the county we're waiting on now."

"The county?"

"The building inspector has to inspect the wiring before we cover it, to be sure it's up to code. Otherwise, you'll never get insurance for this joint."

"You're waiting for him?"

"Sure, that's why I'm here now. Those guys come on their own schedule, and you'd better damn well be here when they are or they won't sign off on the work. Once we get approval from him, we'll blow this pop stand in no time. Of course, we'll have to come back to replace the windows in the room you're using. But that's only a morning's work."

"You could sure do that now if you're waiting for something to do."

"Can't," he said, nodding. "We're waiting for them to come in from the manufacturer."

"You guys sure wait a lot, don't you?"

"Some days are worse than others. You know how it goes."

SHE DID, indeed, know how it went. Her first hour at the theater was spent waiting for God knew who or what. The cast sat and talked and speculated about the delay in the director's arrival on stage. He was upstairs in the executive offices, and the gossip was that management might scrap the production entirely, leaving them to fall back on something from their repertoire to open their season.

Margot was sitting in the third row of the theater with her friend, Connie, when they were joined by her understudy, Anne Lewis.

"Hurry up and wait," Anne said. "God, we could be rehearsing but all we do is sit. I can't stand this."

"Things will move fast enough soon," Margot said. "Take the chance to slow down when it comes to you."

"I don't have time to slow down," Anne said sourly. "You've already made it, Margot, so it's easy for you. But I'm on the bottom rung. I'll never get anywhere sitting around."

Connie laughed. "Relax, babe. You can't rush the management."

"I can't relax until we've been open at least a week," Anne said.

"Sure, but that's about the time vocal strain will raise its ugly head," Connie said to her. "Anyway, you know darn well that Margot isn't going to miss a performance, don't you?"

"You're right." Anne slouched back into the theater seat. "There's really no use in my worrying about this, is there. Margot Wylde has never missed a show and I don't expect that you're going to start now."

"There's always a first time," Margot said, consoling her.

Connie was one of those many singers whom Edward Bellamy had described as being content in the chorus. Anne, however, was not, and it was clear that she chafed in the role of Margot's understudy. She would certainly be a soloist some day, but for now she was doing her apprenticeship. She was only twenty-four, but at twenty-nine Margot could well remember the impatience with which she looked forward to the rest of her career.

"They'll probably scrap the whole thing now," Anne said, pouting.

"No, they won't scrap it now," Connie said, more in hope than in certainty. "They've already advertised it to the hilt. I hear that advance sales are far above normal."

"That's because they expect some sort of gory horror festival," Anne interjected. "If they only knew."

"Don't remind me." Connie sighed.

"It will be all right, I think." Margot remembered Bellamy's confidence and took heart in it. "Edward Bellamy will be able to fix it."

"So he *is* doing the libretto? How did you find out?" Connie sat up, eager for any news to give her hope.

"I paid a courtesy call on my neighbor last night and he confirmed it. He's quite confident that he can give us something that won't be booed off the stage."

"What's he like?" Connie asked. "Is he as cranky as I've heard?"

"Cranky? No, he was quite polite," Margot said. "Downright charming, to a point."

"What point? Did he try to hit on you?"

"No, not at all. I guess the point was that he doesn't like opera. He's doing this for Victor."

"Yeah, a challenge to his bank account. I heard there's a piece of the box office in it for him," Anne said.

"But what is he like?" Connie pressed.

"Tall and dark and very self-assured," Margot answered. "Well, maybe egotistical is more correct." *Yes, perhaps egotistical, but with eyes that swallowed you whole and hands so large and strong that she felt she could hide within their palms.*

"He should be," Connie said. "When the guy writes a shopping list, it becomes a bestseller."

"I've obviously been out of the country too long," Margot commented. "I'd never seen one of his books until last night."

"Maybe you should try to read a book every now and again," Connie taunted her. "Keep in touch with things."

"Not horror, Connie."

"Oh, you're just too cheap to buy one. They've got them at the library, you know. Or I could loan you a couple of his books. You might be surprised."

"I'd be surprised if I made it through a chapter."

Further conversation was cut off by the arrival of the full complement of the opera's artistic staff. Amid the group, Edward Bellamy's imposing figure stood out nearly a head above the rest.

"All right, gang," Daniel Pressman, the director, called out. "Gather around. We've got some business and then you may all go about your petty little lives." Pressman was a smug little stick of a man whose ego, if visible, would have dwarfed his person tenfold. "The weeks of torture are over, boys and girls, for our salvation has arrived." The tone of his voice conveyed that he didn't believe a word of what he had said.

Avery Lister, managing director of the company, pressed past the director then, consternation marking his corpulent features as he waddled up to the stage.

"We're in the process of cleaning up the libretto," he told them as he turned before the orchestra pit to face the company that had gathered in the audience. "I know we're well into rehearsal, but our changes won't affect the music. That has never been the problem. But, as many of you have been so kind to point out, the story is a bit lacking." He paused a bit for the laughter to die down before continuing. "With that in mind, we've hired someone, though new to opera, who we feel can put the show back into shape. Edward Bellamy is here, and he'll have a few words. Ed?"

Bellamy strode up to the front of the group like a Western sheriff about to confront a band of desperadoes shooting up the town. He paused, smiled, and then shook his head in amusement.

"You people have actually been rehearsing this stuff for two months?" he asked. "What a waste. Well, you can forget it now. Any dialogue or lyrics you've bothered to memorize are now to be forgotten, banished, wiped clear from your minds. Okay? I imagine that most of you people could read the reviews when you first read the script. It's damn embarrassing to be closed on opening night, so we're going to save you from that embarrassment."

Several members of the cast applauded and some laughed, but most waited for the reaction of the directing staff, who sat stone faced in the rear.

"Like he said, we won't touch the music. If you were singing in Italian, you might still have a hit, but you're not. I know a person isn't supposed to speak ill of the dead, but I'll make no bones about the fact that Jerome Taylor would never have been my first choice to write anything. I suppose people want to save money, and they probably didn't think a horror vehicle took much talent to write, but there are limits to how low in the bargain basement a person should shop."

There was more laughter on that line, and more stoic silence from the rear of the group.

"Okay, so you can all continue with the music and costume fittings and practicing your sword fights or whatever you need to do, but throw the book away. Boy, I tell you, the music you've got here is just fabulous. Ms. Wylde over there has two of the most beautiful arias ever written for opera. It would be a shame to waste that coloratura mezzo voice or this music on a one-week run. I'll have a new script for you by this time next week. Maybe sooner. You'll have to knock yourselves out to learn it in time, but I make an absolute promise that it will be worth the work."

He cleared his throat then, looking over the group before he said, "I hope there are no questions, because I have no answers. I've never written an opera before, so I've got to go to the library now to research the form. Thank you."

The cast applauded his speech as he walked down the aisle toward the directors, who were getting to their feet. He stopped where Margot was sitting and leaned over to speak to her.

"Find any more masks?" he asked.

"No. Did you?"

"One was enough, it seems. I've been thinking about it, though. Your director mentioned that you've had some minor vandalism over the past couple weeks. A break-in?"

"Yes, but nothing was taken. Why?"

"I don't know. It just seemed strange that just when I'm taking on *The Masque of the Red Death*, a red devil's mask turns up on my patio. And that singing. It sounded like opera to me, though I'll confess that I didn't hear it very clearly. Do you think it means anything?"

"I don't know what it could mean," she said.

"You heard singing, too?" Connie interrupted from beside her. "Margot has been hearing singing for a couple weeks."

"You have?" Bellamy asked. "Where, in the city?"

"Yes, but nobody else seems to have heard it," Margot said.

"She's gotten several telephone calls, too," Connie added.

"I should introduce you two, since Connie has apparently taken over our conversation," Margot said. "Edward Bellamy, this is Connie Dwight. I've been rooming with her, and I'm sure the phone calls were meant for her, since it was her number."

"Pleased to meet you." Connie extended her hand to him, beaming. "The calls only come when Margot is there to receive them. If the calls were meant for me, they would come when I'm there. Don't you think so?"

"I agree," he said, shaking her hand with a broad smile. "And you are?" he said to Anne.

"Anne Lewis. But don't mind me, I'm only the understudy." She, too, shook his hand and then slumped back in her seat.

"You haven't been out singing in people's yards, have you, Anne?" he asked.

"Me? My God, no!" The young soprano was clearly horrified by his remark. "The cold night air would ruin me."

"Maybe we should talk about this a bit more," Bellamy said to Margot. "Maybe over dinner."

"Maybe, but not tonight," she replied. It was hard to turn him down. The concentration of his eyes on hers made it seem as though the two other women had disappeared and left them alone in the theater. Still, she felt that she had to gain some kind of control over their relationship as neighbors.

"Maybe tomorrow," he said. "Meanwhile, I've got to get to work. Good day, ladies. I'm sure it will be a pleasure working with you."

He left them in a silence that was only broken when he was gone from the theater and Connie allowed herself a small squeal of delight. "He's beautiful," she exclaimed. "And you turned him down for dinner? Girl, you've been working too hard."

As THE DIRECTORS walked to the stage to address the company, a man in the back of the balcony laughed quietly to himself. Sitting alone in the dark corner, he was safe from observation while retaining a full view of those below. He loved seeing those opera jerks put down. They deserved it. But his main attention was on Margot. Beautiful Margot.

His Margot.

He'd purchased her album weeks ago, nearly wearing out his CD player's replay function in his study. Now it was time for the personal touch. Soon he would have all that he needed and the world would not need Margot Wylde anymore. She would be redundant.

The man smiled, singing a bit of the now defunct aria. The words didn't matter. Only the voice mattered.

Only beautiful Margot's extraordinary voice had any value at all.

THE MOON was full that night. Its shimmering face hung over the placid waters of the ocean like a benevolent god keeping watch on his sleeping subjects. But even as the moon watched over them, the fog was beginning to form along the rocky coast below the dark lighthouse and its lighted companion to the north. Where the land was low enough, the conspirator mist obscured the ground from the moon's view.

Unlike in the city, where much of the terrain was at sea level, the fog only rarely was able to rise to the top of the cliffs. Tonight it would come within twenty feet of the summit before falling back, defeated by elevation. So the acreage around Margot's and Edward's homes was clear beneath the full moon and the many unsleeping stars.

The man drove to the end of the road and turned where it ended at the forest land. Bellamy's lights were on, so he didn't risk getting any closer to Margot until a night when the moon was obscured or the fog had found the strength to scale the cliff. He drove slowly, his headlights off, until he had turned the corner and was out of sight of Edward Bellamy's windows. Then he switched on the lights of his dark green BMW and sped away in frustration.

The careful sound of his passage made no impression on Edward Bellamy, who was seated at his desk, staring at his computer screen. If it had been a year or two earlier, he might have thrown the monitor through the window in disgust. Either he wasn't as disgusted as he thought or he'd learned a few things in the intervening years, for he did nothing more than curse under his breath and gaze at the words taunting him from the screen.

"Idiot," he said carefully and with great meaning. "Try to find a thought. Okay? One simple thought would do for now. We'll work up to bigger things as we go."

Then he laughed and arched back in his chair to snap the knots out of his spine. *Talking to yourself again? You must be in a real fix.*

He knew from experience that his inability to find the right words was temporary, but the knowledge didn't make it any more bearable. He knew the story; he just couldn't seem to find the words. They were in his head, though, and not on the computer screen before him. Staring at it would do nothing to bring them out, so he stood up and walked to the window to look at the fog-shrouded sea below.

The blanket of fog stretched for perhaps a mile out to sea before it dissipated. It looked as though there was a field of cotton candy between the cliffs and the ocean. The moon lit the entire scene in blue and black, giving everything a metallic sheen. A beautiful night. As much as he hated to be drawn by desires rather than intellect, he walked from the main room and down the darkened hall to the guest room on the south side. From there he was able to see Margot Wylde's home.

The lighthouse didn't look lonely anymore. It looked all too filled with life for his comfort now, and he stood in the dark room wondering what he should do about it. It was probably too late to make a good impression. All he could really do was to continue to bull through as he had been and hope he didn't break anything.

But there suddenly seemed to be so much that might be broken . . .

That woman had more talent in her voice than he could ever find in his feeble words. That was what had him stymied on the script. Finding the words to do justice to that marvelous voice seemed impossible.

One of the things he had always hated about opera was coloratura sopranos. The mere thought of those voices twirling up through needless vocal acrobatics into ranges of sound that only dogs could hear, or would want to, set his teeth on edge. Margot, however, was a mezzo-soprano, a soprano with a lower range than that of the usual stars of opera. Her tone was more mellow, pleasing to the ear, incapable of screeching. Yet she was also a coloratura, one of the fancy singers who performed the arcs and spirals of sound that gave opera its image. Mezzos were rarely able to perform such feats, not naturally, at any rate, and never comfortably. But Margot could. She did. She was wonderful.

And that was why he couldn't seem to write for her. He didn't have the words worthy of those expressive lips.

He could easily write for the tenor, Margot's love interest in the story—the words were already in his heart. He knew something of the burning of an operatic love.

He wished he hadn't met her. And he wished he had better impressed her when he had met her. He hoped she would like him, and yet hoped she would turn him away.

God, how he longed to retain the simplicity of a life without love.

What was she doing right now? He could imagine her in her room—no, probably not her own room if the workmen swarming the house by day were any indication. Her room was surely one of those under construction. But he could imagine her sleeping in some soft bed within the structure so temptingly close to his own. She would be in a silk nightgown—white, he thought—with her hair loose about her on the pillow like a fall of gossamer threads shimmering against the white bed linens. Breathing softly, her dreams caressing her slumber as she lay beneath cool silken sheets.

He could imagine so much about her, and wanted to know so much more. Did she sleep on her side? Which side of the bed did she prefer? And, for breakfast, did she favor fruit and toast as he imagined, or a breakfast cereal? Was she an early riser? Or did she waken in a sullen stupor and struggle until noon?

There was so much to imagine. Too much to ever know. But he couldn't stop himself from thinking about it.

God, how he wished that he could.

MARGOT WASN'T sleeping. She had quit her bed half an hour earlier because there was no sleep in it for her and was prowling around her house, trying to imagine it in its finished state. All she saw were wall studs and tools and dust.

Her telephone rang, a harsh clatter in the empty room, and she rushed to answer it.

"Hello?" There was no response, not even breathing from the other end. "Hello?" she said again. "Who is this?" No reply.

She slammed the receiver onto the cradle, shivering slightly in the night air. The calls had followed her—proving that they had always been intended for her. Why? Who would want to scare her like this?

The telephone rang again. She hesitated, but then picked it up again. "Hello? Hello?" When nobody answered she hung it up quickly. Waiting perhaps five seconds, she picked up the receiver once more and listened—to the dial tone.

"Okay, joker, that's enough out of you for the night." She laid the receiver on the kitchen counter and stepped back as though afraid that it might still ring again. Her hands were shaking, and she twisted her fingers together to stop their unwanted movement.

What on earth was going on? Was Bellamy right in thinking that his devil mask had something to do with it? Margot stood in her dark living room. There could be no answer to something that made so little sense. Why would someone be calling her like that, or singing to her at night? Now that Bellamy had heard singing, too, she could no longer tell herself that it was her imagination, and to think that the singing and the telephone calls were not related relied too much on coincidence.

No, they had to be related to each other and, most likely, to the mask Bellamy had found outside of his home. And if they were, then they must in turn relate to the opera.

She dearly wished that she had remained asleep rather than to be asking such questions. The sound of a car passing slowly had awakened her. She had heard the car drive by but had not seen any corresponding lights, and her sleepy contemplation of why someone would be driving without lights had first brought her to full wakefulness. Now she also wondered about that. Might someone have been trying to pass unnoticed?

But here, too, she might have imagined the sound. It might have been the wind in the trees that had impressed itself on her mind. After all, there was no reason for anyone to drive out here with or without their lights on. And they couldn't very well have called her on the telephone just after driving by, could they?

There was no point to wondering. The phone was off the hook, so there could be no more calls, and she wasn't about to go outside in search of Halloween masks. She should go to sleep. But there was so much to keep her awake. It seemed as though everything was pressing in on her lately, interfering with her normal pattern of life.

She'd signed a contract for the longest engagement she'd ever committed to with the opera. Two years was a vast stretch of time in comparison to her past work. And now she'd put down roots. Was that a rash act? Was she compensating for some other lack by buying such an extravagant house? She suddenly felt unsure of her motives for anything.

It all went back to the fact that for the first time in her career she found herself in uncharted waters. She'd played most of the classic masterpieces of opera as well as many by modern masters, and she'd always come up a winner. What would being associated with an opera that was sure to be attacked by critics from coast to coast do to her career? A bit of a failure always rubs off on the cast, no matter who was at fault. And they'd trumpeted this production so greatly that the impact of its failure would be all the greater.

Now that they'd hired a bestselling author to fix the script, the opera critics would be exceptionally watchful for any defect. They would be looking for any excuse to criticize the efforts of a writer from outside of the club. Her whole career depended on the ability of a literary storm trooper to write a story that solved their script problems—and one perfect enough to keep the critics at bay as well.

On the surface it seemed easy enough to simply write better dialogue and thus save the day. But Jerome Taylor had written the lyrics for the music as well, and they were no better than the incidental dialogue or the story itself, for that matter. Fixing the opera meant rewriting everything so that it would still fit the music.

Could Bellamy do it? Despite Connie's admiration of his work, and her own growing appreciation of the man, Margot had her doubts. But then, it was a Halloween opera, and a horror writer would probably be the best to do it. And he was, apparently, talented. He was a bestselling author, anyway. But was he really any good?

Anne had been right about waiting. It bothered Margot, too. She hated the fact that she was at loose ends until Edward Bellamy finished his writing.

Margot walked into the living room, moonlight shining on her mint green silk nightgown and rippling where the moon fluttered and clung to the contours of her body. She felt out of place in her living room, which looked more like a scene of devastation than construction site by moonlight.

The inspector must have come, for they'd put up most of the wallboards. The room had begun to take on a more finished look with the studs covered, but the glimpses of the structure beneath the smooth surface of the walls was still disconcertingly like a glimpse of the structure of her own life. There was nothing but wood and nails to keep the roof from crashing down on her. They seemed like such frail materials.

Stop that. Find something to get you off to sleep.

She didn't have enough food in the house for a midnight snack, and had no real diversion to tire her. If she lay in her bed, she would only get stiff waiting for sleep.

But she did have something. Connie had loaned her one of Bellamy's books.

Margot smiled. That should make her sleepy.

She took a bottle of mineral water from the refrigerator and returned to the small northwest bedroom she was using. She removed the heavy hardcover book from her oversize purse and propped up two pillows to read by the light of her bedside lamp.

His picture on the back cover had been taken at his home. Her lighthouse was visible in the background. The wind was blowing his hair, giving him a wild and dangerous look, but the black-and-white photograph couldn't capture his eyes.

Those eyes. She could have easily discounted the man as a blowhard if not for the color of those eyes and the way they seemed to be seeing her better than she ever saw herself. The look of those eyes had made her stomach flutter the other evening. And his kiss . . . well, it was best not to think of that.

Margot turned the book over and opened the cover. *Whiteout,* was the title. It apparently had something to do with the Midwest and a snowstorm, but the summary on the dust jacket was very brief. The dedication was briefer still. *For Kay,* it said simply, which caused Margot to speculate on who Kay might be.

But that didn't matter. There was obviously no Kay over there now.

She turned to the first page and began to read.

When the wind whips the snow that has already fallen in a deadly fog over the highway and new snow joins the fray at twilight, life's compass loses its bearings and spins free on its axis until all directions look the same and all are equally fruitless. There is no escape and no progress to be made against it. "Stay with the car," the old timers say. "Stay with the car." And though you run out of gas waiting to come out of the white, stay with the car, stay with what you know is safe. You might be twenty feet

from safety and never make it in the whiteout. And
so might we all be lost, with our outstretched hands
just touching the goal that we could never quite see.

An hour and three chapters later, she was still reading.
She wasn't sleepy yet.

Nor was she listening, for she didn't hear the car return and stop at the woods. Clouds had crept in to complete the job their grounded cousins had been unable to
accomplish. The moon was covered, its light cut by half
so that the shadows stretched long and black across the
ground and the evil that prefers concealment was em-
boldened to act.

The man pressed his car door shut so that it just clicked,
extinguishing the interior light. Then he walked toward
the lighthouse, which stood like a gray obelisk against the
darker gray sky. Seeing the light in the back bedroom, he
skirted the house to the front at the base of the light tower,
where he came upon a window frame covered by a sheet
of plastic. Once there, he began to work quietly on the
staples holding it in place. This wouldn't take long, and
then he'd have her wrapped up tight when he was ready
for the coup de grace.

WHEN MARGOT DID go to sleep, it wasn't because she
wanted to but because she was too tired to keep her eyes
open any longer. She wanted to continue reading, but
common sense prevailed.

The characters had taken on life in her mind, and the
book itself had an insidious way of slipping into her sub-
conscious and making her start at every small sound she
heard. She had been certain that she'd heard someone in
the house earlier, but assured herself it was only the

creeping paranoia of a woman engrossed in a horror novel. Nothing more.

The last thought she had before giving up her grip on wakefulness was of Edward Bellamy's eyes. She felt as though she were falling into them, diving into them as though they were twin pools of cool blue water.

She could think of nothing more refreshing than the sight of his cool blue eyes.

Chapter Three

"If you're going to remove plastic, you should staple it back down again, Ms. Wylde." Tom Gleason spoke laconically through the bare opening for her living room window, his thin form framed against the backdrop of the short stretch of grass and the ocean behind him. "If you'd had a storm last night, the whole place might have been soaked. You're lucky it was calm."

"I didn't take any off. Where do you mean?" A tide of fear surged within her as she spoke. Something had been removed from her home overnight?

Dressed casually in jeans and an old university sweatshirt, Margot followed the workman outside and around to a small window in the entryway joining the house and the light tower. The plastic that had covered the window was fluttering in the light breeze.

"See? It's only plastic," he told her. "A stiff gale would blow it in and all the water with it."

"Hello," someone shouted from around the corner of the house. "Anybody home?"

"Over here, by the light tower," Margot called out. Then she turned back to the young carpenter again. "I didn't touch it," she repeated. "Maybe there was a wind and it tore off."

"No, the staples were pulled out."

"Good morning." Bellamy came around the house and joined them at the window. "What's that about staples?"

"Somebody took the staples out of the plastic covering the window," Margot told him.

"Probably used a pliers," Tom added. "We didn't put it up to be permanent. Looks like there was someone out here in running shoes."

"Bellamy, this is Tom Gleason," Margot said. "He's on the crew."

"Hi," Bellamy said, extending his hand to the other man. "I'm Edward Bellamy, her nosy neighbor. Those tennis-shoe prints probably just belong to someone on your crew."

"No, we all wear work boots. OSHA rules, you know."

"Well, maybe some kids were messing around last night and got scared off when they realized that I was here." Margot was feeling a bit desperate to find a logical explanation.

"But your car is outside," Bellamy said. "They'd have known you were here."

"Yes, they would have, wouldn't they?" She wished that both men would just shut up about it and let the subject rest. It was as though they were determined to scare her.

"You know, maybe living out here in an unfinished house isn't so smart," Tom commented. He sounded sincerely concerned for her safety. "Anybody could get in before we get it sealed up."

"When will that be?" Bellamy asked.

"We'll have the windows in today. The walls will be up and ready for taping tomorrow. I suppose you'll be safe enough tonight, Ms. Wylde. I wonder about this monkey

business, though," he said, flipping the sheet of plastic up
with one hand as he spoke.

"YOUR FRIENDLY CARPENTER might have pulled the staples himself," Bellamy suggested as they walked along the
cliff top a few minutes later.

"Why?"

"So he could show his concern for you." Bellamy
shrugged. "It's a long shot, of course. And the truth is
that I rather doubt it. Did you hear anything last night?"

"No. Well, I thought I heard a noise, and it might have
been someone messing with the plastic, but at the time I
decided that it was my imagination."

"Apparently it wasn't."

"No, I guess not."

The ocean was choppy today; a surface breeze that
couldn't quite reach their elevation was whipping up
ridges of white far below them. Gulls circled overhead as
they watched in momentary silence. The birds cried out to
one another as they floated until they spotted something
worth diving for in the ocean below. Then they de-
scended like bullets to the water and disappeared, then
bobbed up, snapping their meal back into their throats.

"I had a couple of phone calls last night," Margot admitted then. "It rang but nobody answered. I finally took
the receiver off the hook."

"Just like the calls you got in the city?"

"Exactly. I had the impression that he just wanted to
hear me talk."

She looked back at her home, marveling at its beauty.
The base of the tower was about five feet in from the edge
of the cliff, and the structure tapered gracefully to the
glass walls of the room containing the light a hundred feet

above. She estimated the tower's height to be more than that of a fifteen-story building.

It looked deceptively safe in the bright morning sunlight.

"What brought you over today?" she asked.

"I wanted to talk," he said. "And it looks like it's about time that we did have a serious talk."

"I'd offer you some coffee, but I don't have any made."

"I've got some. Let's go to my place."

As they walked, she took time to notice that his eyes were bloodshot and darkened with fatigue. He hadn't shaved, so a dark stubble sprinkled with gray darkened his jaw. In this light she noticed for the first time that there was gray at his temples as well, single strands twining back with the others to highlight his dark hair.

"You're making this seem awfully mysterious," she said as they reached his home. "What is it?"

"Let's get inside first. I want to sit down where I can hear you better."

She followed him into the house, entering an exceptionally large kitchen with a breakfast area flooded with light and a view of the sea.

"It's not decaf," he told her as he poured. "I don't believe in decaf."

"Don't believe in using it?"

"No, I don't believe it exists. I think it's a lie cooked up by the coffee companies to sell the dust they sweep up in their warehouses for big profits."

"Decaf does taste a bit off," she said, following his lead.

"See? That bitter taste is from the sweeping compound." He laughed, sounding almost giddy for a moment as he took his own cup to the table and sat. "You're done remodeling in three days?"

"So they tell me."

"Except for the painting and carpeting and decorating."

"Thank you so much for reminding me, Bellamy."

"You're welcome."

She sat across from him at the mission oak table. "Did you want to talk about my construction? Was that all?"

"No, but I am concerned that you can't lock the place up properly. Of course, anybody who wants to get in can break a window easily enough. Do you have any alarms installed?"

"Goodness, I didn't think I'd need them."

"It would be a good idea. I can send over the guys who did my place if you'd like. Not only for when you're home," he said quickly when he saw the beginning of a refusal coming to her lips, "but if you're going to be out of the country for long periods of time, you'll want something in place to alert the police to break-ins. It'll help your insurance rates."

"Well, that makes sense, I suppose. Yes, I'd appreciate it if you could do that."

"Done. But that wasn't what I wanted to talk to you about, either." He sipped his coffee, unsure of how to proceed. He didn't want to sound paranoid, but on the other hand knew he probably couldn't avoid it. "I found out some things about Jerome Taylor's death," he told her.

"You did? Why?"

"Well, I hadn't intended to, but I wanted to get his notes on the production. I called our agent—we have the same agent, you know, which is part of the reason they hired him. Well, anyway, I called and he said that the police had impounded all of his personal things."

"That's not normal, is it?"

"Not so far as I've ever heard, no. I called the L.A. cops then. They had me on the phone for nearly an hour asking about him and my association with him and the opera. It was a very intrusive questioning, but they insisted that it was standard procedure. It's not."

"So what are you thinking?"

"That Jerome Taylor didn't die accidentally," Bellamy said. "I know it sounds farfetched, but why else did they seal his apartment and seize his effects? Why grill me about how I got the writing gig for the opera? I imagine that they've let the accident story out to avoid too much media speculation and interference. And, I suppose, they're expecting the killer to get cocky."

"Sure, cocky enough to kill somebody else."

"You, maybe," he said seriously. "That's why I was thinking that you should move back to town for a while. Or, better yet, move in here with me. I've got alarms all over this joint, so nobody could touch you."

"Oh, come on, why would anyone want to harm me?"

"Why kill Taylor? We don't need a motive to make us take precautions."

"I just moved in, Bellamy. Now you want me to go running off for protection against...against what? Against a guy who calls me on the phone?"

"A guy who tears the plastic off your window in the dead of night," Bellamy reminded her. "A guy who sneaks around leaving Halloween masks on my patio."

"Both of which might have been done by kids," she countered. "No, I can't just run off and—"

"Okay," he said, raising his hands in defeat. "I didn't expect you to agree, but you can't blame me for trying. I don't think he'd move against you here first, anyway. I would imagine the opera itself would be his first target.''

''The opera? Why?''

''There you go with motive again. We don't know. We can't know. The only reason I can think of for someone to kill Jerome Taylor is to screw up the opera production. Right?''

''I suppose,'' she agreed.

''But killing the author isn't enough. You've got to do a great deal more to get the opera board to drop an expensive production, so he'll have to act at the theater. Killing you out here would look like a separate event, and wouldn't do anything but give your understudy a shot at stardom.''

''But someone removed those staples.''

''Maybe he's building up to something big.''

''But he'll have to do that something big pretty soon. We're only three weeks away from opening.''

''Exactly. Now, if this were one of my books, I'd have him bide his time with little stuff until the opening night.''

''Friday the thirteenth?''

''Right. If you schedule a horror opera to open on Friday the thirteenth, you've got to expect trouble. It would be perfect to lay in a series of minor events and cap it off with a huge disaster on opening night. But, I don't suppose he'll do that.''

''Why not?''

''If he has some kind of grudge against the opera, he doesn't necessarily have one against the audience. I think it's a private thing.''

''Maybe it's someone with a grudge against Victor?''

''Victor?'' Bellamy sat back, surprised by the notion. It hadn't occurred to him that it might be centered on the composer.

"Sure, it's his opera. Has he offended anyone that you can think of?"

"Plenty of people, I'm sure. Narrowing it down might be tough."

"What about just at the opera?"

"Well, as musical director, he's in charge of hiring and firing singers. He's really in charge of all casting, since they hire people for their voices more than looks or acting ability."

"So it may be someone he fired from the company. That would give the person a strong motive to go against everyone rather than just getting Victor himself."

"Right. Destroying Victor's chance to leave a musical legacy would be sweet revenge."

"We should talk to Victor about it," she suggested.

"I'd rather not just yet. He's got enough on his mind. And we can check the personnel records to get any names we might need. Besides, what if it's someone in the current company? If we tell Victor, he'll tell the board and he might be alerted that we're on to him."

"You're assuming that it's a man."

"Yes, of course. But it would be too easy if it was a woman."

"Why?"

"Because the only logical suspect would be Anne Lewis, your understudy. The only one in the cast who has been bothered so far has been you, and she'd be the only one to gain by your death or injury."

"And she surely wouldn't dare talk on the phone," Margot added. "That would account for the singing as well."

"Why?"

"Because it was a woman that I heard singing."

"Could be a high tenor."

"Singing my arias?"

"Okay, so we'll keep an eye on Anne. I doubt that she had the opportunity to fly down to L.A. and kill Taylor, though."

"It could be done, though it does make it tougher. Daniel Pressman could have made the flight, though," she said excitedly. "He was off for three days that week. He said that he had a bad cold, but could have gone to L.A."

"Okay, so we'll put him on our list."

"But neither has any motive to ruin the opera by killing the author."

"No, but they have motive to make it better," Bellamy suggested. "I know it makes me sound like Joe Ego to say this, but my version is a vast improvement on what you had before. Your understudy wouldn't want to become a star of a flop, would she? And Pressman's reputation would suffer from a bad opera. They've got plenty of motive."

Margot laughed slightly, hiding her mirth behind one hand.

"What?" he asked, smiling.

"Joe Ego," she said, shaking her head. "Don't worry, Bellamy, I already knew that you were Joe Ego."

"Only when I'm writing," he said. Then he reached across the table to grasp her hand in both of his, staring across into her eyes. "I don't have ego enough to think that I can protect you alone. And I'd hate to have anything bad happen to you."

"I can take care of myself," she said, though she kept her hand in his and her eyes on his eyes. Despite his doubts, she felt that he could protect her very well indeed.

"Yes, you can, but I plan to worry anyway."

"Why?"

"Maybe I'm hoping for another chance to kiss an opera singer," he said.

"Oh, but you seemed quite able to make your own opportunities," Margot replied. "Or have you become shy all of a sudden?"

"I've rediscovered manners. I'm not sure that I have them down pat yet, though, so you'd better keep your guard up."

"Maybe." She squeezed his hand, feeling as though she might kiss him herself. "Maybe not."

Bellamy cleared his throat, his smile waning somewhat. "Yes, well, I sure don't want to have to get used to another new neighbor, so let's work at keeping you safe. When's the housewarming party?" He released her hand, breaking the spell his touch had put her under.

"What? Oh my goodness, I hadn't even thought about that. Do I have to?"

"What are you, antisocial?" He scowled theatrically. "Make it B.Y.O.B. and it won't cost you much."

"B.Y.O.B.?"

"Bring Your Own Bottle." He shook his head. "What on earth did you do during your formative years, sit in your room playing Maria Callas records?"

"Beverly Sills." She laughed. "You must have spent your youth reading *Mad Magazine's Insults for Every Occasion.*"

"That was a classic," he said. "There isn't a day goes by I don't thank God I read it."

"Boy, aren't we glib." She sipped her coffee, which was very strong. "So, how goes the writing? We don't have much time to rehearse your stuff."

"You guys are professionals," he said. "You can handle a bit of pressure. Besides, you'll have act one tomorrow."

"Wonderful." Relief washed through her like cool rain. "I can hardly wait to sing it."

"Well, you'll have to give me a couple days on your first aria," he said. "The act closer is still on the drawing board, but I've finished most of the rest."

"That's better than I had dared to hope. When did you start work?"

"Last week. But I had to read Jerome's junk and then sleep off the ill effects of it. Then I did some research on my new angle."

"He is dead, you know," she reminded him. "Should you be talking so badly about him?"

"Should I find nice things to say about Hitler just because he's dead? No, and I'm not comparing the two of them, either. But a writer is known by what he writes, and Jerry Taylor didn't leave much of a legacy."

"But he was kind to small dogs, right?"

"No, that was Hitler."

"I give up," she said. "So, what have you changed?"

"Everything." His voice became quite serious when speaking about his work. "Taylor used the title *The Masque of the Red Death* primarily because it provided an excuse for the waltzes in the score and, I suppose, because it sounded spooky. The Edgar Allan Poe estate would have sued him if they'd seen his stuff, however. I know you haven't read the actual story, but it concerns a group of spoiled rich people who lock themselves into a walled fortress in order to escape a plague sweeping through the country. It's the plague that is called the Red Death. It involves a lot of bleeding, you see. Well, they hold a masked ball and the Red Death shows up in human form and kills them all. The end."

"What a sweet story."

"Yes, short, gory and full of suffering. Perfect opera. It's a straightforward and rather preachy allegory. Of course Taylor didn't use any of that, but turned it into some yarn about a ghost at a birthday party. I put Poe back into it."

"His descendants will be pleased."

"I didn't put that much of him back." He finished his coffee and stood. "Probably still more Bellamy than Poe. More coffee?"

"No thank you, I've got about three cups in this one."

"I suppose it is a bit strong. Weak coffee gives me a stomachache."

"Do you do everything contrary to the rest of the world?"

"Only when I think about it. Am I so contrary?" he asked when he sat again.

"Well, opinionated, I suppose. It just makes you seem contrary."

"I was raised to say what I thought. Don't you just hate people who never speak their minds? Wouldn't you like to just club them while they're busy bowing to the opinions of others as if they have no minds of their own? I would."

"Well, there's an opinion." She smiled and finished her own coffee. "So where were you raised to be so bold?"

"New York City."

"That explains nearly everything," she commented. "The eldest son of professional baseball hecklers no doubt."

"Well, maybe when the Yankees were still worth heckling," he answered. "No, they were musicians."

"Musicians?" She hadn't expected that. "So you're not really coming at this assignment without training. Do you play anything?"

"Piano. Used to play saxophone, but that was years ago."

Piano... of course, with those beautiful hands he'd be a natural.

"Any singing in your background? You're a baritone, aren't you?"

"Hey, lady, I've already got a job." He laughed. "And there was no mention of singing in the job description."

"I was just curious."

"What about you? Any creative writing in your past? Poetry, perhaps?"

"No, nothing of that nature. I did take ballet for a while but I grew too tall."

"Ballet's loss, opera's gain."

"Thank you."

"See? Sometimes it isn't rude to tell the truth," he teased. "With a little rehearsal I can be quite a gentleman."

"I don't doubt that for a minute. And, as you pointed out, you are a very good host."

"You could let me prove it," he said quickly, as though suddenly inspired. "Come over for dinner tonight. I'm not a very good cook but I haven't poisoned anyone yet."

"You're just trying to keep me out of my house."

"Sure, but you've got to eat."

"I don't know," she said haltingly. "It wouldn't look good for me to be consorting with the author."

"Why? You've already got your job, too. Six o'clock?"

"I shouldn't."

"I'll shave," he promised. "Probably even bathe. And I won't say anything bad about opera."

"Well, maybe if you promise to play piano for me, I can make it."

"Gee, I don't know." He rubbed one hand over his jaw. "The piano is in my bedroom. That might not be proper."

"I'll decide what's proper," she said quickly. "Do we have a deal?"

"Sure, I'll dazzle you with my 'Chopsticks.' What kind of frozen pizza to you like?"

"No anchovies."

"Nobody really eats anchovy pizzas, do they?"

"Why is your piano in your bedroom?" The idea intrigued her, sounding slightly decadent yet in keeping with the man's no-nonsense life.

"It wouldn't fit in the bathroom." He smiled impishly.

"Oh, of course. No, really, why?"

"Personal reasons," he said simply, still smiling. "We built the house around it and it's too damn big to get it down now."

His voice had chilled suddenly over the subject of the piano, but he was clearly trying not to let it show. Apparently his honesty didn't include revealing the personal.

"I should let you get back to ripping off Edgar Allan Poe," she said then. She stood, noting the slowness with which he rose with her.

"You'll be careful, won't you?"

"Yes, I promise. All I've got is a costume fitting at noon," she explained. "I'll be back shortly after that. You should get some rest."

"Do I look tired?"

"You're one of those people who writes at night, and it's showing."

"Funny, I don't feel tired. I did earlier, but not now."

"You'll need your strength to play piano for me."

"Right. I'll need a lot of strength for that."

They stood looking at each other for a moment, each falling victim to the other's eyes, and then they broke the gaze sheepishly, aware of the spell they'd been under.

"I'll be here at six," she promised as she walked to the kitchen door. "Are we dressing for dinner?"

"Of course. It's considered bad form to dine nude on a first date."

Margot laughed, glad to let him entertain her—and glad to know that he felt the need to entertain her. It made her feel very special.

"But this is California," she said as she stepped out of the house. "I'm not sure of the rules yet."

"You come however you feel comfortable." He stopped in the doorway, leaning against the frame to watch her. "I'll certainly be looking forward to seeing you."

At the edge of his flagstone patio she stopped and turned back. "Say, you didn't say where your parents played."

"No, I didn't." He was grinning again, Cheshire cat-like as he leaned with his arms folded over his broad chest.

"Where?"

"My mother sang on Broadway. Chorus parts mostly," he told her. "My father played second violin in the pit orchestra at the Metropolitan Opera for twenty years. See you tonight."

He ducked back into the house before she could comment, leaving her with a bemused smile on her face. This man grew more complex the more she learned about him. But why did he hate the opera?

Back home the workmen had gone off someplace leaving everything still half finished, but she didn't mind. She strolled through the rooms, examining their work in progress and noting that they had indeed made progress.

As she walked through the empty rooms, she sang through a scale. Then she practiced a few of the trills in her first aria, the one still without words, substituting a long A for the old lyrics. No matter the other problems, the music for *The Masque of the Red Death* was as beautiful as anything in classic opera. She could hardly wait to have the song completed.

The sound of her voice drifted faintly to Edward Bellamy's house, ebbing and flowing on the wind to lull him off to sleep in his reclining chair facing the sea.

Her voice was swallowed in the sound of the ocean below and lost amid the currents of the air, but it came quite clearly across the headphones plugged into the radio receiver in the dark green BMW parked just around the curve of the road. The microphones he'd planted in her home last night did their job admirably, and the man smiled and leaned back in his seat, absorbing the voice.

Her mesmerizing voice.

Chapter Four

"Don't gain any weight or I'll kill you."

Pamela Laurie, the costume mistress, knelt at Margot's feet, pinning up the hem of the beautiful, shimmering red-and-gold gown she'd created for the final ballroom scene. An overworked brunette with a less than cheerful disposition, Pamela saw all actors primarily as hazards for her designs rather than players in a drama. The stage was a platform not for the drama but for her creations, and consequently, she had been known to create gowns that were so cumbersome that they couldn't be moved in comfortably enough to perform the actions the role required.

Her work was stunning, however, and very operatic in its overabundance. The dress she'd made for Margot's final scene was one such extravagant creation. The flamboyant gown was held out by delicate hoops in its petticoat, lifting the full skirt an inch from the floor and holding it just far enough from Margot's legs to ensure her ability to dance and move about on the stage. Apparently, Pamela had learned her lesson in the area of stage movement, but the bodice was another matter. She had cut the strapless gown so low that Margot had to hold it up for the fitting. There didn't seem to be any provision for a support system of any kind.

"Are you planning to put wires in up here?" Margot asked.

"And ruin the lines? Are you nuts?" Pamela spoke around a mouth full of pins. "It'll look great."

"But it won't stay up. This isn't a strip show."

"It'll stay up. We'll glue it."

"I can't be glued into my dress," Margot said matter-of-factly.

"What, you want to use thumbtacks?" Pamela glanced up at her in dismissal. Actors were a nuisance.

"Put straps on it."

"Sing louder."

"What?"

"I don't tell you your business, so don't tell me mine."

"It could have been cut a bit higher, at any rate," Margot continued, conceding the previous point for now. "There's no room for me in here."

"Hey, when word of this dress gets around, they'll be lining up for balcony seats. Hold still."

"This is wonderful," Margot snapped. "It won't cover my breasts anyway, so it doesn't matter if it falls down on stage, does it? How am I supposed to sing if I'm worried about the gown?"

"I told you, sing louder."

"I don't think Daniel will like this." Margot didn't like the idea of using the director's name as a backup to her argument, but she didn't seem to be making any headway with the personal approach. "You can't let the costumes dictate the show."

"Pressman will love the dress," Pamela assured her. "It's your first show here, but you'll see. He'll love the dress."

"He's not a fool. This just won't work."

"Don't be silly, of course he's a fool. Okay," she said, standing. "You can take it off, but don't step on the hem."

"Take it off? Just take my hands away and let it fall off, you mean."

"You prima donnas are a pain in the butt," Pamela said. Then she turned and walked away.

Right about then Margot knew exactly where she'd start if she were planning to kill opera members.

"HAS ANYONE seen my music?" Anne Lewis was scowling as she entered the rehearsal hall below the stage near the dressing rooms. "I left it on my table yesterday and it's gone now. Maybe I don't rate much around here, but you could at least leave my music alone."

The few singers who had come in today shrugged or offered brief negative responses and went back to their own work. Anne turned to Margot, who had just entered, comfortably dressed in her street clothes again. "You don't have my music, do you?" she asked her accusingly.

"No, I haven't seen it," Margot said abruptly.

"Oh, I'm sorry," Anne said, taking a quick note of Margot's tone of voice. "Of course you didn't take my music."

"That's quite all right. I feel a bit snappish at the moment, myself. I just finished my fitting."

"The cherry-tart dress?" Anne smiled. "She put me into that thing earlier. As much as I want to play your role, I'm beginning to hope you never get ill. I'm not nearly endowed enough to hold that thing up if I have to wear it."

"Don't worry, she plans to use glue," Margot assured her. "I'm going to talk to Pressman about it."

"Good luck." Anne laughed. "Cleavage is his first concern."

"That's it, I'm doomed. Well, I can help you, anyway. I've got my music here and you can borrow it until yours turns up. Come on."

The women left the rehearsal area and walked to Margot's dressing room, a space that would have been quite roomy if it weren't for the costumes already hanging on the bar that spanned the room on one wall. A dressing table, couch and two chairs had been crammed into the remaining space, and Anne took a seat on one of the chairs.

"Here." Margot handed the music to her and sat on the couch. "How long have you been with the company?"

"Little over a year. It's my first job," she admitted.

"So you know the ins and outs around here. What's the story with Pamela? Is she always so surly?"

"On a good day, sure." Anne paged through the music as she spoke, studying the lines avidly. "She's one of those people who isn't happy unless she's complaining."

"She'd complain if they hung her with a new rope," Margot commented.

"What?"

"Just something my father used to say. Never mind. Have their past productions been as disorganized as this one?" Margot spoke nonchalantly but watched the other woman closely for her responses.

"No, they're usually efficient enough."

"I suppose the death of an opera's author isn't really very commonplace. The day Taylor died was a Wednesday, I think. It seems as though we had costume fittings that day, too. Do you remember?"

"Lord, yes," Anne responded quickly. "I was so stuffed up that day I could hardly breathe."

"Really? Yes, I remember that now. Pressman had a cold, too, but you did manage to make it into work that day."

"He's a director. I'm nobody," Anne said sourly. "If I called in sick, I'd only prove that nobody would miss me."

"Oh, we'd miss you," Margot assured her, feeling somewhat easier with the woman now. She did remember Anne's cold, though she couldn't be certain that the young woman hadn't caught a flight to Los Angeles right after work. It did seem unlikely, however.

"I've been thinking about seeing some friends in L.A.," Margot said then. "But we're always so busy here. Do you know if there are any evening flights? You know, not too late?"

"Sure, there's a flight every day at five-thirty," Anne replied. "Five or five-thirty. It's a business shuttle. You could be down in L.A. by six-thirty."

"Really? How do you know that?"

"I used to have a boyfriend in L.A.," she admitted. "Thank God that ended, because I sure can't afford the plane fare."

"Yes, it could mount up, couldn't it." Margot felt her trepidations rise again. The woman could easily have flown to L.A. in time to kill Taylor. "Well, I suppose I should get out of here now," Margot said.

"Wait a second." Anne brought the score over to her, turning it with her finger beneath one section as she stood close at Margot's side. "How are you singing this part? I keep getting tripped up."

"Oh, yes, that's a nasty passage." Margot backed up instinctively, keeping some distance between them.

"He wants such a large range in here that it's impossible to shift quickly enough."

"If you have to, you can just brush over the low phrase, but you've got to hit the high notes right on. Here, I've got the tape on that section. I've been practicing it myself." Margot found herself talking nervously as she turned to the cassette player on her dressing table. "It's easier with the orchestra. Here, no—say, that's strange." She hit the Eject button on the machine. The door popped open but there was no tape inside to eject. "My tape is missing."

"Is someone collecting souvenirs around here, or what?"

"I don't know." Margot searched around her dressing table, hoping against hope that she'd put the tape aside and forgotten. "It wouldn't do anyone any good. There's a passage missing and a couple false starts, so it's not as though they could get a decent bootleg of the score."

"Nobody bootlegs opera," Anne said. "It's probably someone in the cast. They have odd notions about community property around here."

"I hope so. It would be the pits to have a thief running around backstage."

"Yeah, they might steal your red dress."

"I wonder what she'd replace it with. A garter belt and bustier?"

"Probably. You know, I hate to ask, but could you run through that passage without the music? I'd like to work on it tonight."

"Sure, but I haven't warmed up. I may not be able to do it either."

"You don't know how encouraging that would be," Anne said. "Sometimes I don't think I'm cut out for this. I'm not sure if I can do it."

"Think you can, and then you can. Another of my father's sayings," Margot said. "But it's true enough. Don't ever doubt your ability. You've got a great voice."

"Thank you, but it can't compare to yours. Your control amazes me, Margot. And you're only a little older than I am! You're scary."

"Please, I get enough compliments from my agent. They made you my understudy because they knew you could sing the part. Don't ever forget that."

"No, I got the part because they know you've never missed a performance in five years. And because I can fit into your clothes. Almost fit." She laughed. "Okay, let me sing it first and you tell me what you think."

The two women practiced together for an hour. Music and laughter drifted out of the room like the sound of a pleasant dream that reached out through the alley door and beyond, to finally be lost in the sounds of the city going about its business beneath a darkening, overcast sky.

Margot sought out Daniel Pressman after leaving Anne, using the matter of the dress to start a conversation.

"The dress is beautiful, dear," he told her, patting her shoulder like a condescending uncle giving advice. "Pamela is a genius. One hell of a little seamstress. If she says it'll work, it will work."

"I'll fall out of it! I can't sing that way!" Margot allowed herself to get mad at the man, something she generally avoided if possible. "Have her put straps on it at least."

"No, we'll let Pamela run her own show, honey," he said. "If we have problems with it at rehearsal, we can make adjustments. You don't trouble yourself with the little stuff. That's what I'm here for."

The director smiled smugly, his narrow face bunching up beneath his eyes like the cheeks of an underfed chipmunk with his mouth full of nuts.

Margot checked her annoyance and smiled. "I hate to say it, but I feel a touch of a cold coming on," she told him. "What did you do to doctor your cold?"

"Cold, hell, it was bronchitis, dear," he said. "I was sick as a dog. I'll tell you, though, it was the only time I have ever been glad that I quit smoking."

MARGOT LEFT the theater shortly before three o'clock, which was well after most of the cast had gone. Anne remained behind, working over the songs with Victor Grimaldi. The man had a lot riding on this show, and he was taking care that everyone involved was well versed in their parts—even the understudies. If it went well musically, his career as a composer would blossom. If not, Victor would become another footnote in opera history.

Daniel Pressman had left the theater just ahead of Margot, and was just entering the bar down the street when Margot emerged. *Maybe he'll find a bottle that he likes and not bother to come out again,* she thought wryly. She, for one, wouldn't mourn his absence.

Margot was free and clear for the rest of the day, free to do as she pleased and having to please no one. Until six o'clock, that was.

She was momentarily tempted to call Edward Bellamy and beg off the meal, but his reference to frozen pizza seemed to mean that he was actually a good cook. It would be like him to pass off his abilities as a joke in an attempt to surprise her with the truth.

Margot couldn't cook a bit. She'd spent her youth studying voice and movement, and any free time she'd had was spent in pursuit of boys rather than culinary skills. Her mother was a fabulous cook, but she'd never seen any value in cooking and so hadn't taught her daughter. Margot's voice was important to Marjory Wylde, not cooking.

Now that she had a home of her own, Margot found herself wishing that she'd learned. Heretofore her work had allowed her the luxury of room service and hotel dinners, and as her snacks generally consisted of raw vegetables, she had no need to worry about it while she was traveling. But she'd have to fend for herself now, and she foresaw a long, blighted life of frozen dinners and delivered pizzas.

As Margot drove home, she tried to put together the facts that she knew into a logical bundle. Anne had been present at the theater the day the writer died, but could still have made it to Los Angeles in time to have killed Taylor. Daniel Pressman was a more likely suspect, however. He'd been gone until late the next day, when he arrived with news of Taylor's death. She wondered about his bronchitis, though. Maybe, if she could get a look at the personnel records, she could find his doctor's name and come up with an excuse to check out his illness.

You're getting to be a regular Nancy Drew, aren't you? she thought. But she had made some progress, and it would be interesting to hear what Bellamy had to say about the information.

Thinking of Bellamy made thoughts of murder and intrigue seem rather distant. It was hard to concentrate on anything but his eyes and the pleasant sound of his voice when she thought of him. She wondered whether tonight he would try for a second kiss. She might just beat him to it.

VICTOR GRIMALDI turned on the piano bench and beamed up at Anne, who stood nervously awaiting his comment on her song.

"Bravo!" he exclaimed, his hearty voice booming out in the empty rehearsal hall. "You glide through that passage much more easily than before. Much more easily. I think you will be a star, young miss worrywart. A big star of international opera. One day, of course. Now you must continue to practice, sleep well and keep warm. And then practice some more."

"I will," she assured him, closing her borrowed score eagerly. "But how can I be sure I'll always hit those notes? They come so quickly."

"Your voice is your muscle, my dear. A weight lifter lifts his weights and a baseball pitcher works out his throwing arm. You work out your voice. When it is strong you can control it. And then, too, you must warm it up before using it to be certain of hitting the mark. The baseball pitcher never goes into the game without working in the bullpen first, you see. So don't be discouraged if your cold voice does not always hit the mark. Loosen up your muscle first and you will be surprised."

"You and Margot make it sound so easy," she said. "Why did you cast me, Victor? I'm not at her level."

"But you will be," he said as he stood. "There can be no carbon copy made of a voice, can there? The understudy is not supposed to copy the lead's performance but to create her own. We must admit that Margot has a wonderful muscle. But even she has limits. Use your own voice and pay no attention to Margot's singing. You are your own singer, my dear, your own weight lifter."

When Anne left him, she was feeling optimistic. She had never doubted her ability quite so much as she had since Margot had come to the company. The fact was that she had been the best of the regular members until then, and, fresh out of music school, she had decided to make herself an essential member of the company. But they'd always filled the lead roles with guest soloists and so Anne had played supporting roles, learning in the process that she was merely a fish of medium stature in a very small pond. Now, they'd hired a truly big fish, and Anne felt very small.

But Margot and Victor were right. She couldn't let the talent of other singers diminish her confidence. After all, she was surely a harsher critic of herself than anyone else could be.

The young singer hurried down the darkened hall to her dressing room for her coat and purse, carrying Margot's score under her arm protectively. As she passed Margot's dressing room, she heard a low thump behind the door and stopped walking. She waited for a moment, listening, and then decided that she'd been mistaken and began to walk away. A creaking noise brought her attention back to the door, however. Someone was in the dressing room, and she'd seen Margot leave half an hour earlier.

Anne reached for the knob of the door but stopped herself halfway. No, she wasn't about to be a fool and confront their sneak thief alone. Victor may still be in the building. And, if not, she knew there were people upstairs in the administrative offices. She'd run for one of them.

But the next sound that came from the room stopped her again, easing her fears. Someone was singing through a scale in a low alto voice. Obviously not a sneak thief.

Anne knocked on the door, smiling. "Margot? Is that you?"

She grasped the knob, turning it and just beginning to speak as she pushed the door open. Then the door was pulled violently inward, jerking her off-balance into the room with a short yelp of surprise.

The next sound from the dressing room was a quickly muffled scream. Then, silence.

Chapter Five

The light rain seemed determined to grow heavier as the evening progressed, if the darkness of the clouds overhead was any indication. Edward watched the steady drizzle from his kitchen window and tried not to think of it as an omen. But he just couldn't escape the feeling that the whole evening was bound to be a disaster.

He wasn't even sure why he had invited her. Or, more correctly, he did know but didn't like his reason. He didn't want to feel this way—not about her, or any woman.

As he watched the rain fall like tears from the sky, he couldn't stop his mind from wandering into the minefield of memory where it probed indiscriminately, daring the bombs to explode.

"You write all the time, anyway, Eddy," she had said, *knowing he hated the diminutive form of his name. "You won't miss me for more time than it takes to slip a new sheet into your typewriter."*

He had tried to protest his innocence, plead his love, and failed.

"No, I've had enough of this half marriage. You brought me out here to the boondocks and you don't even talk to me. I'm just a character in your life, and a small one at that. Well, I've got the lead part in my life, and I'm

going to write it alone from now on." She'd slammed her suitcase shut and hefted it from the bed. "Don't worry about alimony. I haven't received anything from you yet, so there's no sense starting now!"

The last thing he'd said as she hurried through the door was her name. It was the last thing he ever said to her. It had echoed in his mind for three years, though it rarely passed his lips. He was almost afraid that saying it aloud would unleash a bolt of lightning over his head.

"Kay," he said now, quietly, like a prayer for absolution. Nothing happened.

"Margot," he said then, smiling. "Margot Wylde."

Saying her name brought a lump to his throat, making him feel happy—if only briefly—before his thoughts darkened to consider the matter of her window. He didn't trust that carpenter. Perhaps he'd been in the opera company and had taken this construction job for the sole purpose of getting closer to Margot. The man had a forced friendliness about him that might indicate a nervous sort of infatuation with Margot . . . or be a sign that he was covering up more sinister plans.

"WE GOT the windows in," Tom said as he packed the rest of the tools into a massive tool chest in the middle of Margot's future living room. "Walls up and taped, windows in and most of our mess cleaned up. It looks like we're ahead of schedule."

"This is wonderful," Margot told him. "I guess I didn't expect you to actually finish."

"Have you been upstairs yet?" The young man spoke eagerly, grinning as he stood.

"No, why?"

"The walls are already primed up there," he said. "We cleaned up the hardwood floors, too. You could move up there to sleep if you wanted to."

"That's great! You guys are miracle workers."

"You want some help? We could move the bed up if you want to sleep upstairs tonight," Tom told her. He stood shifting from one foot to the other in happy nervousness. He clearly wanted her to appreciate the work they'd done. "It wouldn't be any problem."

"No, my furniture isn't here yet, so there's no point moving that single bed up."

"Gonna get a double, huh?" Quickly, in embarrassment, he added, "Sure, 'cause it's a huge room. About the size of my apartment."

"You've done enough for me already." She was suddenly inexplicably uneasy being alone with him. The man was too eager. "I don't want to keep you from anything."

"The only thing you're keeping me from is the bar." He laughed. "Not that I go there every night. Couldn't pound nails all day if I did."

"I understand. You've finished a big job and it's time to unwind before the next one. We do the same thing in the opera."

"Yeah, I suppose you guys party down big-time. It must be fun."

"It's a job," she said.

"Yeah, right." He laughed, seeming to imagine a vast gulf between his life and hers. "Say, you should be sure to keep your new windows locked up good. Remember those tennis-shoe prints outside that window this morning. Somebody tore that plastic off on purpose."

"Oh, come on. If it was anyone it would have been kids. That's nothing to worry about."

"Maybe, but lock up, anyway. I could stop by later to see that you're all right."

"I can take care of myself," she said, a bit more forcefully than she would have liked.

"Oh, sure, I know," he said quickly. "I just meant that I'd hate to see anything happen to you living out here alone like this." He began walking toward the door as he spoke, aware now that he'd overstepped the bounds of friendliness. "Hey, you just enjoy your place. We'll be back tomorrow to finish up some odds and ends."

"I will enjoy it. Thank you," she called as he stepped through the door. "See you tomorrow."

Margot was sorry that she'd snapped at him like that, but he had made her nervous with his own nervousness. And his continuing talk about her being alone out here seemed sinister. She hoped that he would not come by later, especially if he'd been to a bar. It was the quiet, nervous type that a person had to watch out for—especially when that type had been drinking.

They needed to check up on him if they could. His employer would have some kind of background on him—enough at least to tell them if he'd ever had any connection to the opera. There were carpenters on the stage crew, after all.

She stood for a moment in the center of the room and listened to the thrum of rain on the roof. The living room walls were bare, unpainted Sheetrock with smeared lines of plaster-coated tape covering the seams between sheets, creating a white-on-white motif around her. The room echoed when she walked, the sound of her heels on the wood floors joining the sounds of the rain.

She *was* alone out here. Though Bellamy lived close at hand, he was still too far away to stop a determined assailant. The distance between their houses was suddenly apparent to her, making her shiver with dread.

The telephone rang, its echo jarring her harshly. Margot walked quickly to answer it.

"Hello?"

"Ms. Wylde?" said a rather high, unaccented male voice on the line.

"Yes."

"I missed you at the theater," he said. "Maybe next time."

"What?"

The man hung up, leaving Margot standing with the drone of a dead line in her ear.

What on earth was that all about? He missed me?

The bare white walls seemed to press in on her like a box, a trap that had fallen around her. She shouldn't be here alone. Bellamy was right about that. She should be safe within his security system rather than sitting here like a target.

Stop that! This is your home!

She resolved to be strong and face the situation squarely. Bellamy was right in saying that it didn't make sense for the man to move against her right away. If his target was the opera itself, he would surely want to concentrate his efforts in the theater . . . wouldn't he?

Margot went from room to room, casting a critical eye on her new surroundings. It seemed brand-new to her now, all smooth and finished. The only room they hadn't done was the room she had been using, and that was because it was the only room she hadn't wanted changed. Its walls still showed the cracks brought on by time and use, the paint carrying dim smudges from past occupants. The room occupied the northwest corner of the house like a ghost haunting the new construction.

After assuring herself that the ceiling lights all worked and the windows did open and shut—and lock—she climbed the open stairway leading up to her bedroom suite.

She'd had the entire second floor converted specifically for her use. A large bedroom with a bathroom containing a sunken tub and separate shower filled the eastern half, while a music room took up the west with a breathtaking view of the sea beyond its windows. There was a fireplace, and soon there would be bookshelves and an Oriental rug covering the fine original oak flooring.

She could imagine it as a sunny, friendly place, but right now it was an echoing and empty chamber, more like a warehouse than a home. For the moment, she preferred the old, used room she occupied. She could escape from the ground floor more easily than she could from up here.

Having finished her tour, Margot went back down and ran water in the tub of the downstairs bathroom. They had replaced the fixtures and window but, as with the one bedroom, hadn't done the walls because there was really no need for any change. Now her island in the sea of chaos had become an island amid a vast echoing emptiness. And she much preferred the chaos to this frightening lack that made her feel so vulnerable.

FROM THE MOMENT Margot stepped through the door, damp from the misting rain still darkening the world around their two houses on the cliff, Edward Bellamy had been courteous to a fault.

The meal was a bit of a surprise, and not because of any pretensions but rather for its lack of them. Serving a simple tossed salad and crusty bread to start, he'd followed with a beef roast, new potatoes and asparagus.

"So you don't think Anne did it?" he said over the meal.

"No, I said that she was there that day. But she could have gotten to L.A. in plenty of time to kill him," Margot said. "But let's not talk about that yet. Okay? I'm enjoying myself."

"You are?" A smile broke over his face, as though her enjoyment was the most important thing on earth for him.

"Yes, I am. Let's not spoil it."

"No, you're right. We've got the whole evening. You know, I should have asked what you liked to eat. You might have been a vegetarian."

"It's a lovely meal," she told him. "I'll have to ask you to give me some pointers."

"I doubt that I could tell you much."

"But you're assuming that I know how to cook." Margot smiled at his mistake.

"You can't?" He tilted his head quizzically. "I guess that's what you might call a gender blunder. Men do tend to assume that women know how to cook."

"I've never had a need to cook. Where did you learn?" she asked as they went into his main room for wine.

"Here and there," he said, pouring two glasses. "I worked in a restaurant kitchen once a long time ago. The chef was an ex-navy cook. A crotchety old semiliterate drunk, if you want the truth, but boy could he cook. I figured that if he could do it, I could, too. Mostly, I learned how to read cookbooks."

"Is there a trick to it?" She sipped her wine.

"It's a matter of learning the terminology. Knowing the difference between sautéing and frying is a big step."

"Even I know that," she said, and laughed.

"See, you're halfway there already." His smile faded. "But cooking doesn't get us any closer to figuring this thing out, does it?"

"No. And I don't suppose we can avoid the subject. But we can't really discover anything either, can we? Both Anne Lewis and Daniel Pressman had opportunity to kill Jerome Taylor, but probably lots of other people did, too."

"Right," he admitted. "But if the killer is connected to the opera, that narrows it down quite a bit."

"But is he currently a member of the company?"

"We'll check on that tomorrow."

"But we can't do anything tonight."

"We can keep you safe," he said. "That's something."

"I can't stay here, Bellamy. It wouldn't be right." But her heart picked up its pace at the prospect, and she found herself regretting the words even as she said them. Her independence couldn't be as important as her life.

"But I'll catch cold sitting out in your yard all night."

"Oh, come now. You won't do any such thing."

"I will if you don't stay here where you're safe. Come on, I can have a security system put into your house tomorrow. Humor me for just one night."

"Oh, I suppose I could," she said, allowing a smile to steal onto her lips. "But only to save you from illness."

"Thank you," he said, grasping her hand in his. "I wasn't looking forward to camping out."

"But no more wine for me," she told him. "I've got to keep a firm grip on reality."

"Don't you trust me?"

"Yes, I do. Maybe I don't trust myself."

"And maybe you shouldn't trust me, either." He laughed. "Okay, we've got that out of the way. So, what are people supposed to do after dinner?"

"They talk, generally."

"Right. Small talk." He nodded his head as though the notion of small talk was new to him. "So, how did you get into the opera business? Did your folks start you out?"

"Not really. I was just one of those kids who couldn't seem to stop singing. After a while, my parents stopped begging me to be quiet and consulted a vocal coach to see if I had any potential."

"And the rest is history. They must be very proud."

"Yes, but the nature of my work means that they don't see me perform very often."

"Will they be here for the opening?"

"Yes, of course. I'll probably have two rows of relatives in the front of the theater. What about you? What did your parents want you to be when you grew up?" she asked, wanting to shift the subject away from herself.

"They wanted me to be an accountant."

"No, really?"

"Sure, it's a dependable profession."

"Where theirs weren't? But your father was twenty years with the Met. That's pretty dependable."

"It was a job, anyway." He scowled slightly, finishing his wine to mask whatever emotion his face might have revealed. "So what do you think of the San Francisco Modern Opera? Does it measure up to world standards?"

"It's fair enough. There's a lot of talent there, but little direction. To have allowed the *Masque* to go into rehearsals in the shape it was in wasn't really very swift."

"They had no choice once they'd advertised." He laughed. "The show is supposed to be some great Halloween extravaganza to bring in fresh audiences. But it's the well-known operas that get the crowds in town, not this one, and the company's on the verge of bankruptcy."

"Why on earth did they commission a new opera if they're in such bad shape?"

"Victor was going to take his music and hit the road. They figured that if they mounted a production using his music, they would keep him happy and on staff and save a few bucks in the process."

"Mounting a new opera is hardly a way to save money."

"But it's a modern opera," he explained. "If you call something a modern opera, you can get away without building sets. Unfortunately, until now, most of the stuff they've done has really been glorified musical theater."

"So their big premiere is nothing but a gimmick?"

"No. I'm sure that someone up there had good intentions somewhere along the line, but hiring a clown like Jerome Taylor to put words to their music shows a distinct lack of sense."

"Why didn't they hire you at first? Victor wanted you to do it."

"They wouldn't pay my price." He smiled broadly. "I would have done it quite reasonably for Victor, but he was in no mood to humor them after all the wrangling they went through over the music. I'm not cheap—especially for opera."

"You promised not to say anything bad about my work," she cautioned him.

"I could never say anything bad about your work," he said.

His smile was gone then, replaced by a look of rapt attention and absolute sincerity that nearly made Margot blush with its intensity.

"So," she began, trying to cover the sudden trembling of her heart with words. "So, they ended up with you, anyway. What did they have to pay?"

"A piece of the action," he said. "A big piece. Once they go into profits, that is."

"That was foolish, wasn't it? They'll probably never go into profits."

"Gee, I knew I should have gone into accounting. Are you sure you won't have more wine?"

"No, but thank you. So, you do all of your work in here?" Margot stood and walked toward his desk as she spoke, looking over the notepads and other papers scattered by his computer. "Doesn't the view distract you?"

"Since I work at night, there is no view." He joined her at the window.

"The night must agree with you. You've done very well. What do you do for fun?"

"I write."

"Nothing else?"

He looked out of the window over the dark expanse of ocean. "It's what I do."

The sun had just set, the splendor of its disappearing light hidden by the clouds. The lower portion of the window was slightly open, and she could hear the surf pounding unseen against the rocks below the cliff. It would be a melancholy sound to work to, hypnotic and sad.

"I see that you have quite a collection of music here," she said, filling the sudden void with a reference to the small shelves near his desk that were filled with CDs.

"Some of your family's musical taste must have rubbed off on you."

"Some. I suppose that's why I took this job." He spoke without looking away from the window, his gaze fixed on the sea barely visible beneath the wan moonlight. "Grimaldi did a fantastic job. It's modern and classical by turns, and there's a hint of jazz to it. A truly modern operatic score. But he doesn't know anything about dramatic plotting. If you don't have a plot you've got nothing."

"Oh, I think there's a bit of singing going in, too," she reminded him.

"All wasted if the audience is asleep or headed for their cars before you get to the showstoppers."

"I probably shouldn't say it, but I didn't think the lyrics were that bad. The dialogue, well, I guess I agree with you about that, but the songs were good."

"I'll give the devil his due and admit that Taylor did a good job on the songs. But the plot was horrible and the dialogue between songs was like something out of a classic comic book. The plot, the story, is number one."

"But you didn't have to rewrite the lyrics, did you? Couldn't you have just fixed up the story a bit?"

"I don't 'fix up' stories," he said turning toward her. "And I don't put my name on anything I didn't write. Jerome Taylor was paid—which was the only reason he wrote, anyway—but, dead or not, he's not going to have his name on this opera."

"It's a matter of pride."

"I'm a writer," he told her seriously. "That's all I do. It's what defines me. And I won't be defined by anything that isn't as good as I can make it."

It was clear from the way he spoke that he did, indeed, take great pride in his work. From what she'd read, he had a lot to be proud of, too. His work, like the man, had a depth that she hadn't expected to find. She could understand that a man who wrote the way he did couldn't bear to take credit for anything that had even a drop of another man's talent in it. He wouldn't feel honest if he did.

"I don't understand one thing," she said. "Why don't you like opera?"

"My father hated the opera," he said, a faraway look in his eyes. "Like father like son."

"But he—"

He cut her off by placing his hand on her cheek, stroking lightly down to her jawline and pulling her gently toward him. He kissed her with no more warning than that, and their lips lingered, savoring the contact between them.

"Whoops," he whispered, drawing back an inch from her lips. "So much for trusting me, huh?"

"Yes, well, we are neighbors, after all." She sighed, letting her face drift toward his until her lips returned to the warmth his had provided. She felt as though she were floating, her body suddenly light and suspended on a warm breeze that might never let her fall.

The ringing of the telephone on Bellamy's desk cut off the breeze, jarring her back to earth. He shrugged and stepped back with obvious regret. He walked over, snatched up the receiver quickly and answered with a curt "Hello."

He listened for a moment, frowning. "I think she'll want to come in," he said at last. "We'll be there in twenty minutes."

"Where?" Margot asked when he hung up the phone. "What happened?"

"We can scratch off one suspect," he said, his face drained of color. "Anne Lewis was attacked. They found her in your dressing room."

Margot stared at him in shock. The multitude of questions racing through her mind left her entirely without words.

"She apparently disturbed someone in your dressing room slashing up your costumes," he told her, answering her questions while provoking more. "The police think he might have thought she was you."

There was nothing else to be said then. But, for a single guilty moment, Margot couldn't help but wonder what would have happened if it had been *she* who entered the dressing room.

"*Ms. Wylde*," she remembered now, "*I missed you at the theater. Maybe next time.*"

Maybe next time.

Chapter Six

The rain had stopped, which was a blessing considering the way Edward Bellamy was driving as they sped along the twisting road toward San Francisco. At one moment his headlights would be sweeping over the trees and grasses growing on the slope of the hills above them, and the next moment the light touched nothing at all as the curve of the road made it seem as though they were about to launch out over the sea that lay invisible below them. The speed of his driving and the many unanswered questions about Anne's fate made the whole thing unbearable for Margot.

"Slow down, Bellamy!" she exclaimed at last. "We want to see her in the hospital, not join her."

"I'm not going...well, maybe I am." He lifted his foot off the accelerator somewhat. "Nervous, I guess."

"I'm worried, too," she said. "What on earth could have happened?" She hadn't mentioned the call yet, wanting with all of her heart to think that it was a crank call and had nothing to do with the attack on Anne Lewis.

"Grimaldi wasn't very specific," he said grimly. His face, lit by the dashboard, had a deathly pallor to it, and the muscles of his broad jaw were clenched tightly. "He was a bit frantic."

"No doubt. I just hope she's all right."

"I missed you at the theater...." No, don't think about that. *"Maybe next time."*

That call had nothing to do with it. It couldn't. But what else could he have meant? Was there another logical meaning for his words? None. Still, Margot kept her silence, trying to maintain the hope that the man who attacked Anne wasn't waiting for her even now.

The countryside gave way to suburbs, and they joined the many cars on the highway headed toward the bright lights of the City on the Bay.

"She'll be fine," Bellamy said. He reached over to grasp her hand, taking it lightly in his at first, then grasping it more firmly with a consoling squeeze. "If it were really bad, even Grimaldi would have known. Right?"

"Probably," she admitted. Though she couldn't help feeling pessimistic about the young singer who had so recently begun to open up to her. She was glad to know Anne wasn't involved in the Los Angeles author's death, but she wished there had been some other way to find out. Now she felt guilty for having suspected her.

If she was attacked because of me... She couldn't contemplate such a thing without being demolished by guilt. The killer was after the whole company.

"Anne's probably only in for observation," he told her. "She'll be caterwauling like the best of you in a day or two."

"Caterwauling?" Margot found herself laughing suddenly, nervously venting the tension within her with mirth. "Why do you hate opera?"

It was important to speak of other things until they could find out the truth about Anne and either put their fears to rest or have them realized. And Margot could think of nothing better to talk about than the man at her side.

"My father wanted a position with the symphony," he said. "He spent twenty years complaining about singers and operagoers and directors—especially directors. He said he was 'playing background music for a bunch of fat bums to scream over.' I guess you'd say he had a bad attitude. And I never did like opera."

"Did your father ever join the symphony?"

"No. He's dead."

"I'm sorry."

"He was probably destined to be disappointed by life. A very melancholy man."

"How did he die?"

"Car accident. Of course, when you've got a quart of Chivas in your belly, it's probably not fair to call it an accident."

She didn't know what to say to that. There was obviously much more to the story than he was willing to tell, and she wasn't about to force him. Her attempt to lighten the mood with conversation hadn't worked very well.

"My mother still lives in New York," he continued quickly. He turned off the freeway into the city as he spoke. "Wouldn't move away from the theater for anything. I offered her a home anywhere she might want to live, but the only place she'd think of living was the city. I got her a place just off Central Park."

"That's very nice of you."

"Hey, she's my mom. What should I do, leave her in her old rent-controlled walk-up? Of course, I damn near had to kidnap her to get her out of that place. She's stubborn."

"So which parent do you take after?"

"Both, I'm afraid." He laughed lightly, tipping his head to smile at her. "I tend to get stubbornly melancholy."

"An attractive quality in a man."

"Some people don't think so." His smile tightened, and he turned the wheel with a bit more force at the next corner. "Just a block away, now," he said. "Well, at least it stopped raining."

But the moisture in the air hung heavy and damp, coalescing into a low fog that built upon itself until it began to rise through the streets like a slow-moving animal. Soon, it had begun to cloud the view of most of the city's streets. While they were in the hospital, it attempted to crawl up the cliff below the lighthouse as well.

"SHE'S RESTING NOW, and I don't expect there to be any complications," Anne's doctor told Margot just outside the young singer's door. Bellamy had just dropped her off so he could park. "But it would help if you could do something to calm her down. She's worried about her voice." The doctor raised one concerned eyebrow as she frowned. "She won't rest and won't believe my medical opinion at all. She might believe you."

"About what? I don't even know what happened to her yet."

"He choked her quite badly, I'm afraid, and her larynx is swollen. She can barely speak."

"And she's afraid that she won't be able to sing?"

"Exactly," the doctor said, nodding.

"Will she?" Margot asked, feeling in her own heart the same kind of dread that Anne Lewis must be feeling right now. "Will she be able to sing?"

"We can't tell anything until the swelling goes down. But if she doesn't rest, if she continues to talk and aggravates the injury, the swelling won't go down. It may get worse.''

"So I've got to lie to her to calm her down for you.''

"If she will calm down, you won't be lying,'' the woman said. "She's been asking for you since Mr. Grimaldi mentioned calling you. Just talk to her.''

The doctor left it at that, and Margot paused a moment outside the door to collect her thoughts. The poor girl must be beside herself with fear of losing her career, her entire life, in one act of violence. Putting a smile on her face, she turned the knob and opened the door slowly.

Anne lay in the lone bed in the room. The lights were low, and the room smelled of antiseptic, adding to the ill look of the woman in the bed. Her face was turned away from the door, but her cheek was pale and scratched near her ear, and her hair was strewn about as though she'd been thrown backward into the bed with great force.

Margot stepped in, letting the door swing shut behind her, and crossed to the bed. "Anne,'' she said softly, thinking that the young woman might be asleep, and not wanting to wake her.

Anne jerked her head around, fear opening her eyes widely as she sought assurance that her visitor wasn't another assailant come to do her harm.

"Margot,'' she cried out then, her voice nothing more than a rasping whisper. She shifted in the bed to face her visitor. "Somebody was in your dressing room,'' she said. "He just pulled the door open and—and...''

"Don't talk,'' Margot cautioned her. Anne's throat was abraded and puffy, showing bruises where the man's fingers had taken hold. She was also badly bruised beneath her left eye as well as scratched in several places. Just looking at her made Margot feel immensely sad. She pulled a chair to the side of the bed and grasped Anne's hand in hers. "You've got to rest your voice, dear. Don't try to explain or talk about anything. Just rest."

"But when I don't talk, my voice goes away entirely," she said urgently, half rising in the bed. The hospital gown slipped away slightly as she moved, revealing the top of a large purple bruise on her chest. "I can't lose it, Margot," she said, tears welling up in her eyes. "Not now. I'm so close."

"I know." Margot rose to sit on the edge of the bed and put her arms around Anne's quavering shoulders, letting her nestle against her shoulder like a small child seeking comfort during a storm. "You'll be fine," Margot told her. "But you can't recover if you don't let it happen. He injured your throat, so you've got to let it heal on its own."

God, how she must be suffering, Margot thought. *It must seem as though everything is lost. Her whole life gone.* She would have cried herself under the same circumstances. And, no matter what the doctors or anyone said, she would never have believed their assurances about her voice until the day she heard it for herself.

"I thought it was you in there," Anne whispered against Margot's shoulder. "He was singing."

"He was?"

"Yes." Anne pulled back then, using her fingers to wipe the tears away. "Or, somebody was. It sounded like you."

"Don't worry about it now," Margot said. "Don't talk any more."

"But..."

"But nothing. Just keep your mouth shut." She placed two fingers on Anne's lips in emphasis.

The other woman nodded, smiling bravely.

"Good. And if you'll just shut up for a couple days, your voice will come around again. You don't know what kind of permanent damage you might cause by forcing it." Margot stood, smiling. "I've got to find Bellamy, but I'll be right back."

"Bellamy?" Anne croaked. Then she smiled, putting her hand over her mouth.

"Yes," Margot admitted. "We drove up together. You rest a moment and I'll be back."

Margot hurried from the room and down the hall where Bellamy was talking to a pair of men. One of the men turned as she approached, revealing himself to be Daniel Pressman.

"Margot," he said. "How is she?" He approached holding his hands out to grasp hers. "I only just heard and rushed over."

"She's badly bruised," Margot told him, enduring his embrace, "and her voice is gone at the moment. The doctor says that she'll be fine."

"Good, good. I hate the thought of anyone being attacked in our theater. It's horrible. But you, my dear, out on a night like this?" he said, shifting gears effortlessly. "We cannot risk such a fine voice to the elements, can we? And you have no understudy now, either."

"You don't know that."

"No, but neither do I know that we do have one. We can't afford to lose you to a cold, Margot. You, of all people, should know that."

"Don't worry, Pressman, she knows what she's doing." Bellamy stepped between them, a look of amusement in his eyes. "Besides, she's got a voice that would bounce back from anything."

"Oh, yes, and you are an authority," the director said, sniffing slightly. "I'm glad to have your assurance."

"Well, I've seen enough opera singers over the years to realize that overprotectiveness is just as bad as carelessness."

The third man, who had been quietly listening to the three of them, stepped forward now and addressed Margot.

"Miss Wylde, I'm Sergeant Steve Terry. We're investigating the incident. Could I ask you a couple questions?"

"Certainly." Margot shook the hand he offered to her. "I don't think I can help very much, though. I was gone when she was attacked."

"Yes, but the fact was that her assailant was in your dressing room. He was cutting up your costumes."

"He what?" Pressman shouted out in alarm, practically grabbing the policeman in his distress. "He ruined costumes?"

"I'm asking Miss Wylde the questions," the policeman said calmly. "You can visit the costumes at the precinct, if you want to. We're going to have the lab go over them and then you can have them back."

"You can't keep them," Pressman continued. "My God, man, we've got a show to do."

"And I've got questions to ask. Excuse us, please." Sergeant Terry touched Margot's elbow lightly, prompting her to follow him farther down the hall and away from the worried director. "He sure got riled about that bit of news."

"Costumes cost money," she told him.

"And singers don't?" The detective shook his head, amazed.

"What can I help you with?" They stopped midway between the two men and Anne's door, the detective turning so that he could see the men at the end of the hall.

"Do you know of anyone who would want to harm you personally?" He spoke calmly, his voice devoid of interest.

"Me? No, of course not. Do you think he was after me?"

"I never think until I'm done asking questions," the policeman said. "So you have no enemies?"

"None that I can think of. I tried to think of anyone all the way up here, but I couldn't. Well, I don't suppose that everyone in the world loves me, but I can't imagine anyone wanting to harm me."

"Why were you trying to think of people who might harm you?"

"Well, she was attacked in my dressing room, right? I mean, it seemed logical."

"And you could think of no one," he said, shrugging as though he didn't quite believe her answer.

"Nobody," she said dismally.

"What about the opera itself? Have they fired anyone lately? Someone with access to the building?"

"I don't know. I only started with the company in June, and no one's been let go since then."

"That seems to be the way everyone remembers it," he commented. "And you're sure there's no one out there who holds a grudge against you personally?"

"I can't be absolutely certain, but I know there's been no one locally. I've been out of the country for the better part of two years."

"Has anything else happened around here? Anything suspicious?" He seemed disappointed with her answers, as though he'd expected her to be able to solve the whole thing for him with one interview.

"We seem to be missing some music," she said. "Anne's score was gone this afternoon, and a rehearsal tape was taken from my tape recorder in my dressing room. We don't really know that they were stolen, just that we can't find them."

"That could be our man," the officer said. "He may have been there for simple vandalism and she caught him in the act."

"Of course," Margot said in relief. She much preferred that answer to her own. "No one has cause to harm any of us."

"There's no cause to vandalize your property, either," the policeman remarked. "I would suggest that all of you keep on your toes. The next time someone meets this guy, they may not be as lucky as Miss Lewis."

"He probably won't be back."

"No, probably not. People who destroy things for fun don't like to get caught."

"Nobody likes to get caught," she corrected. "Is there anything else? I promised Anne that I'd be back soon."

"No, nothing for now. Take care."

"I will," she assured him. Then she paused, suddenly realizing she had to speak up. "Sergeant, I had another reason to be wondering about people who might want to harm me. Really, I've been trying to convince myself that it meant nothing, but that can't be true."

"What is it?"

"I had a phone call this afternoon. At home," she said. "A man called and said that he missed me at the theater this afternoon. 'Maybe next time,' he said. That was all."

"Just that he missed you at the theater?"

"Yes, and then 'maybe next time.' I didn't think much of it at the time. I sometimes hear from admirers who get all tongue-tied and can't really say much. I thought that was all it was."

"But now you think otherwise."

"Yes, but I still don't think there's anyone specifically trying to get me. I think you were right about this. I think that someone is trying to get even with the company, or maybe they're trying to stop this particular opera. I'm singing the lead, so of course he'd want me rather than my understudy."

"But once he got you, he'd want your understudy, too," he observed. "That's possible, and it would be consistent with stolen rehearsal material and the shredded gowns. You live out of my jurisdiction, don't you?"

"Yes, south of the city."

"I'll alert the sheriff's department. They can run a patrol by your place from time to time just to keep an eye out."

"I would appreciate that," she said. "And you should call the Los Angeles police, too. The opera's author, Jerome Taylor, died two weeks ago. It was supposedly an accidental death, but that doesn't seem likely now. In fact, Mr. Bellamy spoke to the L.A. police and got the distinct impression that they don't think it was accidental, either."

"Yes, I doubt it, too. You've helped quite a bit, Miss Wylde. More than I expected, for that matter, but I don't think you've made it any easier."

"Good luck."

"Same to you. I would advise you to try not to be alone too often. This guy isn't going to want to mess with more than one person at a time. Good night, Miss Wylde." The policeman continued down the hall, having apparently decided that Daniel Pressman wouldn't be worth the effort of talking to any further. Margot returned to Bellamy and the scowling director.

"How is Anne, really?" Bellamy asked her.

"I think she'll be just fine."

"Good," Pressman cut in. "We can't afford to lose anyone at this point. I shan't be staying, then. There's really no point. Good night all," he told them, nodding curtly. Then he walked away quickly without any further word.

"He didn't seem very worried," Margot observed.

"No, not as worried as he should be," Bellamy said. "Did she see who attacked her?"

"No, it happened too fast."

"Then Pressman's still on the list. It would do wonders for ticket sales if the production is known for having a crazed killer stalking it."

"People have certainly been killed for less," Margot agreed. "I think I should stay with Anne for a while," she said. "She's all wound up, and could use some company."

"All right." A small frown formed on his lips. "I could come back for you if you'd like."

"I'll call Connie and stay the night at her place." She reached to touch his arm, instinctively needing to make contact with the tall man before her. "Don't worry, I'll be safe in town."

"I know, but I'll miss you."

"I'm afraid that your piano recital will have to wait until another night." Margot strained to keep their conversation light. The memory of their kiss asserted itself too strongly for her to trust herself with him just then.

"No loss," he commented. Bellamy raised his hand, almost touching her but withdrawing it before he did and stepping back. "I had a wonderful evening."

"Me, too. Remember, I want cooking lessons."

"Anytime. Well, I should go so you can get back to her."

"Yes, well, good night," she said.

"Do you need anything from home?"

"No, I've still got plenty of things at Connie's to see me through. I'll call her to pick me up when I'm ready to leave."

"Okay, then, bye."

It was so awkward a parting between two people who had so suddenly come under each other's spells that they didn't know how to express their feelings. And it was made all the more awkward by the fact that neither of them was entirely certain how they had envisioned their evening concluding.

"Bellamy," she called when he had reached the elevator. "Could you check my house? I'm not sure if I locked the door."

"I'll stop by," he assured her. "I'll see you in the morning."

The elevator doors hissed open and he stepped in. Her last sight of him allowed her a glimpse of a frown darkening his features as the door slid shut between them. Obviously, he didn't like this parting, and that pleased her.

Slow down, she cautioned herself. *You can't let your heart get ahead of your head if you want to maintain your bearings, girl.*

Still, slowing down was the last thing that she wanted to do.

THE FOG WAS dense along the ocean, totally obliterating the road in places. Edward Bellamy drove in silence at first, but when it became obvious that he wasn't going to be able to travel at his accustomed speed, he turned on the car CD player, letting the disk already in place begin.

Margot began singing the lyrics of a Cole Porter song after a brief orchestral opening. She was singing it up-tempo, the way Cole Porter had originally sung it, and her voice was so perfectly suited to the song that it seemed to have been written for her.

She didn't sound like an opera singer singing show tunes at all, which was a definite plus. He'd seen the old films of opera divas from Porter's time singing popular songs and none of them could seem to get rid of their vibrato. None, for that matter, seemed to have any true sense of rhythm.

Margot, however, had a feeling for the music. If she ever tired of opera, she could surely be a star as a jazz singer. Her phrasing was excellent, hitting just behind the beat in the manner of Billie Holiday and making it sound as though she'd invented the technique.

Listening to her sing, he was no longer annoyed at the fog or the car's slow pace. He wanted to close his eyes and drift on the gentle breeze of her voice, letting his cares float away.

As he climbed higher on the road toward home, the fog fell away and his foot began to exert more pressure on the accelerator. It was natural for him to drive fast, for he didn't drive for the sake of driving but rather for the sake of getting someplace. Even with Margot Wylde on the stereo to make the journey pleasant, he couldn't overcome his need to be done with it.

"Slow down! You don't have to drive like a maniac just because you've got a sports car!" He could almost hear Kay's voice in the seat beside him. Earlier, when Margot had pointed out his excessive speed, he had begun to recite his usual response. *"I'm not speeding, dear. Besides, this car handles very well."* How many times had he and Kay repeated that dialogue to each other in the car? How many times had they gotten on each other's nerves while driving?

The fact was that neither he nor Kay could stand to be the passenger in a moving vehicle. Both wanted control of it. Kay quite often drove faster than he when she was behind the wheel.

He turned off the stereo and drove in silence again. It wasn't possible to listen to Margot and think of Kay, not while traveling on the road that had claimed his wife's life.

As the road clung to the edge of the mounting cliff, he drove faster, skidding on the curves as though daring the laws of gravity. *She'd probably been angry when she went off the cliff. Angry at me.* If he'd been willing to concede to the divorce, she would have gotten back to the city safely.

She'd be alive today if he hadn't been so stubborn.

And so he drove faster still.

A YOUNG MAN was stumbling back to his pickup truck from Margot's house when Bellamy's car skidded to a halt on the gravel driveway beside it. He got out of his car ready to confront the man who might well have put Anne into the hospital earlier.

"What the hell are you doing here?" Bellamy's voice boomed out over the sounds of the surf below them.

"I'm a guy who's been working on her house. Said I'd check up on her tonight. Just to be sure she's all right. She's not here." He came up and stopped two feet in front of Bellamy. It was obvious from his swaying and the droop of his eyelids that he was worse the wear for liquor.

"She's in the city. What were you doing in there?"

"I wasn't 'in' anywhere," he said, slurring his words badly. "I told her somebody was trying to get in, but she didn't believe me. Not her. She's not a scaredy-cat." He shook his head, grinning. "So what are *you* doing here if she's in the city?"

"She asked me to make sure she locked the place up. Did she?" Bellamy relaxed somewhat; the boy was drunk and he could easily handle him if he needed to.

"I don't know," he answered. "I didn't try the door. Just knocked. I don't break into people's houses even if I was the guy who did the finished work on the lady's bedroom. That don't give me any rights."

"No, it sure doesn't. I see a light on, though. Are you sure you didn't go in—maybe to use the bathroom?"

"Naw, I used the ditch on the way. So where is she?"

"In the city. I told you. She won't be back tonight."

"I guess I done my good deed then," the young man said. He walked around Edward, fumbling in his pocket for his keys.

"You're not driving anywhere, are you?"

"Suppose not." He leaned against the side of his vehicle. "I can sleep in my truck. Since she ain't coming back, she shouldn't mind, huh? Besides, I gotta be here in the morning anyway."

"Okay, I suppose that's all right," Bellamy agreed. He had almost given in to a humanitarian impulse and invited the man over to sleep on a couch, but the last thing he needed was a drunk in the house. The guy was sleepy now, but who knew what he'd be an hour from now. Besides, if he ran the heater, he'd be comfortable enough in his pickup. "I'm going to check the locks and then I'll be out of your hair," Bellamy said. "But I'm going to keep an eye on the place from my house, so you better plan on staying in your truck."

"Yeah, right," the boy said as he opened the door and slipped in behind the wheel. He started the engine and then closed the door. A moment later, he disappeared behind the dash as he settled into his night's lodgings.

Bellamy hurried down to the lighthouse and first checked the door to the light tower itself. It was locked, but the door to the house was open. He was about to close and lock it again, but thought better of it. He might as well go in and check things properly.

It was going to be a nice place once she had it painted and decorated. He had been inside a couple times before and could appreciate what she'd done with it. A floor lamp was on near the fireplace and, after switching on the overhead light switch by the door, he walked over to shut it off.

She had taken out one of the downstairs bedrooms to make the living room larger. The staircase going up was near the center of the room, and you could walk around and under it. Beyond that, in what had been the bedroom, was a large fireplace. A loop of wire was barely visible hanging down inside of it, and he paused for a moment, contemplating its use. Probably part of some kind of electronic flue, he decided. Bellamy turned off the light and went to the kitchen to check the back door.

She had opened one wall of the kitchen to create a serving bar and updated all of the appliances in there as well as adding a small laundry by the back door. It was all very efficient now.

He smiled. If she really couldn't cook, she'd need all of the efficiency she could get.

As he stood in the kitchen, he thought he saw a brief flash of movement beyond the window. A white blur, nothing more—it might have been a reflection of the light on the glass, but it bothered him. He hurried to the kitchen door and threw it open. There was nobody outside, but he walked out of the house anyway and hurried to the carpenter's pickup truck to check on him.

Inside, Tom Gleason was lying on his back with his legs tucked up against the passenger door and his mouth hanging open in sleep. He couldn't have gotten back that quickly.

You're just jumpy, Bellamy chided himself. *He's passed out.* But he decided to do whatever he could to check up on the fellow in the morning. Drunk or not, he had been snooping around.

Bellamy returned to the kitchen. On his way back, he noticed a book lying on the counter. He recognized the dust jacket even in this dim light as that of his own book *Whiteout.* He noticed, too, that she was halfway through it.

Suddenly, he felt awkward and embarrassed about entering her home so blithely. It didn't matter that her things weren't here; it wasn't a matter of potential embarrassment over his seeing something he shouldn't, but a matter of privacy itself. No matter how much he might yearn for the right to enter her home at will, it was her home, and he had no more right here than a burglar might have. Not yet, anyway.

It wasn't as though she'd invited invasion, as he had when he'd written *Whiteout.*

He left quickly then, locking the door and then double-checking it behind him. He walked all the way around the house testing the windows to assure himself that no one had tried to break in. When he was certain that everything was secure, he hurried up to his car. The carpenter was still curled awkwardly in the front seat of his pickup with the engine running. He wasn't going to be any problem tonight.

I should never have written that book, he thought as he drove home. But he had written it, and dedicated it to a wife who wouldn't have been impressed by either the dedication or the book's painfully autobiographical nature. No, she wouldn't have cared, even if she had lived to see its publication.

But now it was being read by a woman who he wished above all others would have a good opinion of him. The only woman besides Kay for whom he'd ever felt the torturous pains of love.

About twenty minutes after Bellamy was in his own house and back at his computer, the light in Margot's living room came on again. It was on for ten minutes.

Fifteen minutes after it was again extinguished, Tom Gleason's pickup drove away.

Chapter Seven

"Someone has been bothering with our props, and I for one don't think it's a bit funny."

Daniel Pressman stood on the stage before the rather subdued cast of *The Masque of the Red Death*, all of whom had taken seats in the audience for the first read-through of the new script. "We're missing two of our death masks, and they weren't all that cheap to manufacture. I don't know what kind of games you people want to play, but please return the masks as soon as possible. All right then, I'll turn you over to Mr. Bellamy for the read-through." He nodded curtly toward Bellamy and relinquished the stage.

"All right, boys and girls, it's story time. I'm sure that Mr. Pressman would have mentioned that Anne Lewis is doing just fine if he hadn't been distracted by the mask problem," Edward Bellamy told them. "But she is all right. The only danger she's in now is from hospital food, and if someone would volunteer to take some chicken soup over at noon, we can probably ward off that peril, too."

Margot tried to laugh at his joke, as did a couple other friendly souls in the theater, but their hearts weren't in it.

"Meanwhile," he continued, "you had all better watch your backs. Somebody is screwing around here and he seems to be willing to play rough. Don't stay late after rehearsals, okay? And don't go too far away from the rest of the cast."

The cast members immediately fell into an excited buzz as his warning sunk in. What they all feared had finally been said out loud by someone, and it was as if his words had given them all permission to speak. It took a couple minutes for Bellamy to quiet them again.

"We have to concentrate on an opera here," he told them. "If we don't keep on task, Anne won't have a job to come back to. Okay, I've arranged for your various managers and potentates to play someplace else during our meeting, so we should be safe from unwanted opinions during the read-through. I'm not a playwright, so I'm not used to being present when people read my work for the first time. This is really the only chance of bashing my work that I plan to give you. After this morning, you are all contractually obligated to believe that this is the best opera since *Carmen* and to behave accordingly. Also, after this morning, I don't have to show up anymore. Well, almost no more. Any questions?"

"Why do you think Anne was attacked?" someone called out.

"What am I, a psychic?" Bellamy laughed, scratching his fingers back through his hair. "Well, I think someone is trying to stop the opera. We don't know why, but the police are working on it."

Margot stood up then, saying, "If anyone here can think of someone with a grudge against the company, it might help the police if you gave them their name."

"Right, probably somebody who was fired," Bellamy added.

"What on earth are you people doing?" Daniel Pressman walked near the stage. "We're wasting what little time we have left to get this production underway. Don't forget that we open in less than three weeks. I think the police can handle their own work while we handle ours. Let's get to work."

It was clear the Pressman wanted to get through reading the script as soon as possible so that he would be in charge once more.

"Danny's right," Bellamy agreed snidely. "We don't want the police to solve this thing too quickly, do we? It might cut down on the advertising value of the attack."

"What on earth are you implying?" Pressman exclaimed.

"Just that you're an ass, Daniel. Go stand in the corner and we'll do the read-through."

Pressman didn't reply but stood fuming for a moment while the company waited for him to explode. Finally, he walked back and took a seat in the front row.

Bellamy began his explanation of his revisions.

"The story of the Red Death, according to Edgar Allan Poe, is about a plague ravaging a country, and how the prince of the country and a bunch of his friends lock themselves up in a fortress to avoid the disease. Of course, it gets them anyway.

"We begin with a young woman who is not an entirely sympathetic character—a greedy woman—who meets and weds a very wealthy man. The man of her dreams, so to speak. He loves money as much as she does, and far more than he loves her. They learn to overcome their shallow selves, of course, but there's still the small matter of the death waiting outside their walls. The story was originally an allegory about the waste and greed of Poe's time, and I've brought it back to that.

"Except that this time there's music. And though my words can't compare to Grimaldi's score, I can hope that they serve to interpret it."

He paused to sip from the cup of coffee he had been neglecting in his hand. He winced, saying, "I see that theater coffee hasn't changed since the last time I tasted it."

THE STORY was every bit as grand as Bellamy said it would be, with a measure of humanity and understanding that would not have been expected from a conversation with the author. This man clearly understood the pain of love and how addicted people were to it. He understood life.

Beginning comically, with a case of mixed-up packages bringing a poor woman together with a wealthy young man, the story grew with their doomed relationship until all humor was gone. By the time of the masked ball at the conclusion, an air of mystery and dread hung over every word. The ultimate horror of the story was the prospect of a life without love, a horror so great that it consumes them. The plague, finally, is not a disease but a loveless society.

Margot found herself dabbing at her eyes by the end of the read-through, and was heartened to see that several of the cast members were similarly affected. Poor Connie Dwight was weeping openly.

"All that remains to be done are the two arias," Bellamy said. "Robert's second-act closer and Margot's finale. So, comments? Complaints? What do you say, do we have an opera?"

The cast burst into applause. Yes, they had an opera.

REHEARSALS BEGAN again in earnest that afternoon. Daniel Pressman, who may have been a lot of things but was not ignorant, began changing the blocking of their movements on stage to fit the new circumstances with inspired boldness, and the cast reacted quickly to his changes. The new lyrics were taken aside and studied by the principal singers, who tried out the phrasing of the new words to their music. Lighting personnel began to make adjustments as well, and Neil Roberts, the stage manager, went through his copies with highlight markers to chart the arrivals and departures of the actors on stage.

The changes were not all greeted cheerfully, however. David Trierweiller, the temperamental tenor who played Margot's love interest in the play, made no effort at politeness when he confronted Bellamy about the change in his part.

"You've turned my character into a prick!" he shouted out when the author joined him and Margot in their small rehearsal room. "There's not one redeeming characteristic to him!"

"He falls in love with Marie, doesn't he?" Bellamy smiled brightly, obviously prepared for this objection.

"That's hardly a redeeming characteristic," the singer scoffed.

"What are you?" Bellamy asked. "Are you an actor or a star? A singer or an ego with a voice?"

"Show me a good reason for the character to have changed."

"For the good of the plot," Bellamy answered. "All else is second to the plot, and if a heartless corporate raider serves the plot better than a mindless Lothario, then I'm happy to change him. It's your job to play the role, not write it."

"I wouldn't have written him as a fool."

"He's no fool. He's got some meat on his bones now, that's all. You can give him humanity if you're up to the challenge. He shows it in his love. Look at Margot's part. She's not complaining about playing an opportunistic social climber."

"It's her opera," David scoffed.

Bellamy's voice hardened, cutting off further dissent. "An actor plays the part and makes it into something worth watching. A star complains about the number of lines he has and how unsympathetic his character is. You just have to decide if you're an actor or a star."

He left them in awkward silence. David stared at the door with his mouth half-open and Margot discreetly studied her score. Finally, after a tense moment, David turned and said, "Well, I suppose we should begin learning this stuff so that we don't look too foolish."

"That's going to take a lot of rehearsal," was Margot's quiet comment.

Connie, of course, was nearly delirious with happiness over the changes. Not only had Edward Bellamy managed to improve the opera, he'd increased the number of solo roles in the process and she had gotten one of them.

"You better watch it," she said when Margot emerged from the rehearsal of her duet with David. "Today I've got a verse, tomorrow I'm taking over the whole thing."

"It couldn't happen to a nicer person," Margot told her, giving her a big hug as she did. "Victor told me, and I couldn't be happier for you."

"Now all I have to do is get used to the idea of singing alone on stage. I've never had a solo," Connie admitted. "In fact, I'm not really sure that I ever wanted one."

"This is your chance to find out."

"I'm already scared."

"Don't be, Connie. Remember, somebody has to be the lead alto around here."

"But it doesn't necessarily have to be me." Connie laughed, hugging Margot again. "But it's silly to even think about that. I've got a solo right now, in this opera, not next year or the year after. You've got to help me."

"I'll do what I can. After I've got my furniture in place, you can come out to stay a few days. We'll practice all night."

"Just like we did in school."

"Exactly, complete with popcorn."

"It's a date, babe. But I've got to run now. They're changing my costume now that people are actually going to be looking at me, and I've got a fitting. Bye." The woman nearly skipped away in her excitement.

Margot marveled at the change that had overcome the company. Bellamy's script had given them hope. Now, if they would only catch the man who seemed determined to take the hope away, everything would be perfect.

Margot especially wanted the uncertainty taken out of her life. Now that she'd discovered the wealth of feelings that Bellamy had brought out in her, she didn't want to waste time before exploring them.

"THESE COSTUMES are shot." Pamela Laurie was pulling the torn dresses from the box in which the police had returned them when Margot got to her dressing room. "Some pathetic schmuck is going to get his private parts handed to him on a hot plate if I catch up with him."

Margot laughed. "That sounds painful," she said.

"Redoing the costumes is painful," Pamela said. "What I'll do to him will be fatal."

"Are they really that bad?"

"Worse. He cut them through the underlayers, so there's no support left to build on. My crew is going to be working overtime and complaining to high heaven. What the hell did you do to get this guy pissed off?''

''Me? I didn't do anything.''

''That's not what I hear. Most folks figure it was some European psycho following you around. I don't doubt it for a moment. They're all psychos over there.''

''Well, I think I can assure you that I didn't bring this on us. Besides, *who* is saying these things?''

''Everybody. You know this cast, they gossip like they sing. Loudly.''

''And you spread it around?''

''What else have I got to do besides repair four dresses for this show and Lord knows how many that were just hanging here because they were your size. And then I've got a new dress to do for Dwight.''

''Hey, there you are, Laurie!'' Pressman peeked his head in through the door. ''How are they?''

''Shot to hell, what did you expect?'' Pamela dropped the bundle of dresses back into the box. ''They're rags.''

''Damn expensive rags.''

''Still rags. Is that all you want, Danny, because I've got better things to do.''

''No, have you seen the ceremonial sword?''

''Yeah, I took it home to slice salami. It's a prop, so check with props.''

''They don't have it.''

''And neither do I.'' The costumer brushed past him into the hall.

''Say, there was something about Margot's dress, too,'' he called after her. ''Could you put straps on it?''

''That's absolutely last on my list, Danny,'' she shouted back as she turned the corner toward the wardrobe department.

"That woman acts as though she's alone down there," he said to Margot. "It's a shame that she's too good to be fired."

"Why do you need a sword?" Margot asked him.

"We're going to do the regressive progression literally," he told her. "We start in the present and regress into anarchy historically. Swords and all that stuff."

Pressman's eyes held a different look this afternoon, the look of a man with a mission. "It's very exciting, actually. We're scrapping the last set entirely to do the whole thing with lighting. Have you read the Poe story? It's very visual, all about lighting and color. We'll have the stage stripped down to nothing by the finale. Just you and David. Death, too, of course. God, I hope we don't have to make new masks. The fellow who designed them is charging us fifty dollars a copy."

"Wow, that'll strain the budget," Margot commented. "Who is playing Death?"

"Grimaldi is casting that part. It's really just a walk-on. You'll love it—though I suppose that your dress should have as little as possible to it. Theatrically speaking, that is, though we must contend with gravity, mustn't we?"

"I'll let Pamela decide how to handle it," Margot offered. "She's got her hands full now."

"Yes, that she does. Well, I'd best be off. It's nearly opening night, dear one," he reminded her. "And we've got four weeks' work to do."

As THE COMPANY fell into the swing of rehearsal, the man seated in the last row of the balcony could feel the difference as well as anyone on the stage. It was his business to be tuned in to such things, and he was very good at his business.

He was impressed by the changes, but not so impressed that he might be compelled to change his own plans. No, his work was proceeding on schedule and he must continue. There would be no opera. He wouldn't allow it.

While he sat watching the blocking rehearsals and planning his own arcane movements, the sun began to descend beyond the overcast covering the city. Soon, it would be glorious night once more.

Soon, their fine opera would lie in ruins.

THERE MUST BE something better than this, something tangible that can be held on to and savored and doesn't cause such pain. There's got to be something better than love.

But Edward Bellamy could think of nothing better or worse than the feeling that had been growing in his heart since meeting Margot Wylde. He could remember that only days ago he had not felt this way, and he had liked it. He had enjoyed not being in love and not feeling this cold knot in his stomach. The absence of this pain was, in retrospect, pleasurable. He could have gone his whole life without it.

But now that the pain was there, he couldn't live without it. It defined him. It was what made his life worthwhile, and assured him that he was alive.

"When you're away from your typewriter, you're like a zombie. You'd think you were married to a keyboard rather than me. Damn you!"

He pounded his fist down on his desk suddenly, upsetting the half-filled cup of coffee so that dark fluid soaked into the pages of typed manuscript beside the computer monitor. Bellamy watched the pages wrinkle and darken as the coffee soaked up through them, not attempting to stop the flow. It didn't really make any difference. Nothing did. Since Kay's death, love could never be anything but pain and no one could change that fact.

No, someone *could* make a difference. Margot made a difference.

He wished he had been able to find some damning evidence against the young drunken prowler, Tom Gleason, when he checked up on him today, but there had been none. He was a carpenter, nothing more, and he had worked for his current employer for two years and the one before this for three. Aside from drinking too much, there had been nothing bad to find. He had seemed like such a good suspect, too.

Bellamy tried to force the matter out of his mind and concentrate on his work, but he only succeeded in thinking about Margot again. She mesmerized him, and he didn't want to ever come out of her spell.

He was still at his keyboard when he saw the lights of Margot's car sweep past. Knowing that she was home made it harder to work. He couldn't decide if it was more sensible to continue staring fruitlessly at the monitor or to call her on the phone. Or should he go over there?

No. He could have cursed himself for suggesting a security system. Bellamy would rather that she was safe with him here, but that couldn't be helped. The company had already wired in a basic system, enough anyway to sound an alarm should anyone try to get in. Later, they would upgrade it to connect with the local police and provide it with a backup battery system, but they'd done enough on short notice to make her safe there.

No, he wouldn't go over there. He should finish his work. He was writing for her, after all. He was writing for Margot.

SHE PARKED her car, took out two bags of groceries and, after pushing the door shut with one foot, hurried along the walk to the house. It was a chilly night and the clouds created a feeling of gloom that seemed impenetrable as the first of what would be many raindrops began to fall. If she wasn't in such a good mood, the night would seem unbearably bleak. But, with the opera's sudden renewal, she couldn't feel gloomy or even very cold tonight. She felt like celebrating. Perhaps a piano recital would be nice.

Margot put the groceries down on the ground and unlocked her front door. Then she switched on the light, picked up the bags and carried them into her kitchen. On the wall beside the telephone was the small switch box for the security system. Margot flipped the switch just as the security man had instructed and was rewarded by the red glow of the ready light on the panel. There, safe and sound.

The room was finished, with the base coat of paint already dry on the walls. Tomorrow there would be a new flurry of activity as the painters arrived to color her rooms with the tones she'd labored over choosing. Then the carpet installers would arrive, and soon after them, the vans from the furniture stores. In three days, she would be able to unpack the boxes she'd stored in the base of the light tower and truly call this house a home.

After putting her groceries away instead of wandering through the house imagining what it was going to be like when it was all finished, Margot picked up the half-finished novel from the kitchen counter and opened it to the page she'd marked with the flap of the dust cover.

I missed you at the theater. No, she wouldn't worry about that now. He couldn't get at her now. She stared resolutely at the book before her.

For Kay, it said on the first page, *E. Bellamy.* She hadn't asked who Kay was. She wasn't sure that she wanted to know. She had begun to feel slightly jealous of this Kay, whoever she was, because Bellamy was impressed enough with her to dedicate a book to her.

Someday, Margot thought, if the fates were willing, he might dedicate a book to *her.*

She took some fruit into the small bedroom she had been calling home the past couple days and settled down with the book and her tidy little meal while a misting rain began to fall outside. Thunder provided tympanic accompaniment to the wind.

Since she was in for the night, she decided to get comfortable and slipped out of her blouse and slacks. With one look to be sure the curtains were drawn, she took off her bra and slipped her nightgown over her head. That was better. She removed her anklets and slid up on the bed until she was nestled comfortably in the pillows bunched against the headboard. Popping a grape into her mouth, she picked up the book and found her place again.

Burton stood at the head of the stairs and watched his front door sway in the wind, eddies of snow wafting in over the entry carpet in miniature drifts while each gust carried her voice to him. He could not go down there to close that door. No, as much as he wanted to assert his masculinity by bravely marching down the stairs and closing the door, he just couldn't do it. Not when she was down there calling his name. Not when she might catch him down there, defenseless.

He turned in the mounting cold and shuffled back to his bedroom and the bed that had never been warm since she left.

Margot fell back into the story easily, finding the plight of the initially obnoxious lead character quite engrossing. Even a shallow man such as this one was a human being, and he didn't deserve the torture he was going through as his house lost power and the subzero cold of the snowstorm crept in on his last earthly refuge. He was alone in the midst of nothing, totally defenseless against the elements beyond his walls. Alone.

She was alone, too. She, too, was cut off from civilization—and someone out there meant her harm.

Stop that! You're no more than a quarter mile from Bellamy. But it was hard not to draw parallels with her own situation as she read.

She bit into a pear, catching a bit of juice that ran down her chin with one finger. Then she resolutely took up the book again, eating as she read.

The wind was picking up, whistling below the eaves and beginning to take on its own melody as she read of colder winds in a more northern climate of the soul. *Whiteout* was the story of a man with much to atone for, whose actions and inactions had led to sadness and suffering for those around him. And just as he was figuratively blind to his own callousness, the weather becomes literally blinding as a blizzard descends on the farm in which he lives, bringing with it all the ghosts of his past deeds to drive him insane.

Laying the book down open on her lap, Margot ate green grapes and listened to the melody of the wind outside. If she closed her eyes, she could imagine herself on the deck of a clipper ship making way for San Francisco with the guidance of her tower's light. A ship laden with silk, perhaps, for the ladies of the city; or maybe a ship heading out with its hold full of California gold. All of that was in the night's song.

Thoughts of song took her back to the opera. The theft of the masks and the sword showed that their phantom was stepping up his campaign. The sword's being stolen was especially worrisome because it was quite real, though a bit dull, and could certainly do some damage.

She wondered about the singing she had heard in the mist. How could a woman be mixed up in this? They knew for certain that the culprit was a man now, but she had heard a woman's voice singing. Bellamy's suggestion that it was a high tenor just didn't fit the voice she'd heard. It couldn't be possible that they were being threatened by more than one person, could it? Could two people share the same obsession to such a point as this?

Bellamy had checked up on Tom Gleason and hadn't found any connection to the opera. But the young carpenter could very well be involved with a woman who'd been released and held a grudge, so there would not have been any connection to the opera for Bellamy to uncover.

As she pondered the many possibilities of the threat against her, it seemed that she could hear a more ordered melody in the wind outside. A sound like singing—a woman or young boy singing in the night. As she listened, the song coalesced into a more meaningful tune, forming words that she could almost recognize.

With a growing sense of dread, she realized that she did indeed recognize the song. It was her first aria from *The Masque of the Red Death,* in which she sings of her bleak life and the lines that poverty has put into her face. A vain song, self-pitying, but very much in keeping with her character at the beginning of the opera.

She could hear it clearly now, the song drifting to her like the voice of a ghost lost at sea. The killer was out there right now!

Margot got up carefully, marking her place in the book, and walked toward her telephone in the kitchen. A cool breeze was flowing through the rooms at about foot level, not a good sign for supposedly finished construction.

Margot sneaked into the dark living room. There was no curtain up yet, and she would be a perfect target if she turned on the lights. Even in the dim light of the night sky she could see the problem immediately. A window was open.

Had she opened it? She didn't know. Although the security company had assured her that the alarm would work whether windows were open or not, the thought of an intruder's having such easy access chilled her more than any breeze could. She walked over to close it, not daring to make a sound.

The rain was falling more heavily now, and flashes of lightning within the cloud cast bursts of spectral illumination on the ground below. Between lightning flashes, there was a seemingly absolute absence of light. Utter blackness separated her home and the glow of the kitchen lights at Bellamy's.

The lightning flashed, stretching brief shadows from the bushes toward her window. A second flash, and there was... what? A third flash—yes, a man not ten feet from her window. He was wearing one of the masks, a malevolent red face covering all but his mouth and jaw and carved with lines of pain. He raised his arms, lifting his black opera cape like a bat unfolding its wings. Its red satin lining glistened in another flash of light.

But on the next burst of light he was gone.

Maybe next time.

Margot jumped back, staring openmouthed at the window. Had she really seen someone? Her earlier feeling of ease seemed foolish now as the reality of her situation burst through the bubble of illusion she'd built around herself. What did it matter that she had every door and window wired to keep intruders out when they could smash through and kill her before Bellamy could react to the braying sound of the alarm.

Exploding into motion, she closed and latched the window and moved carefully to the center of the room. More lightning revealed nothing. There was no one out there now, but she stood in the darkness peering out first one window and then the next, her skin crawling with the presence of unseen eyes. Nothing. There was no one there.

You shouldn't read horror novels.

No, that wasn't the answer. She *had* heard singing and she *had* seen the man outside. She wasn't fool enough to believe it was just her imagination.

Margot walked to the phone, tiptoeing as quietly as possible even though she knew he couldn't hear her footsteps from outside. She picked up the phone and was about to dial when she realized that she didn't know Bellamy's phone number.

Okay, so turn on the light and look it up in the book.

There was no way around it, so she turned on the kitchen light. Nothing happened. No one jumped out at her, no one screamed or came crashing through the window. She took the telephone book out of the drawer and found his number.

Outside, added to the rumble of thunder and the wind's sad song, was the sound of a pickup truck, unheard by the woman inside the house.

Margot punched Bellamy's numbers, then lifted the receiver to her ear to await the ring. There was nothing.

"Oh, damn it!" She depressed the button to disconnect her call and then put the instrument back to her ear. It was dead.

Outside, the song began again. A clear voice cut through the wind for a moment and then was swirled up in it again. It was her aria, the second one this time. But then it was gone, leaving her wondering if she'd heard it at all.

But she knew that she had heard it.

And she saw light spilling over the lawn outside her window now, too. Car lights.

Margot held her breath for a moment, listening. Yes, there was something. There must be a vehicle out there.

She slipped quickly into the other bedroom, her feet crunching on the slight residue of plaster dust on the floor. Standing to the side of the window, she peered out. Yes, there were headlights gleaming in her backyard, but the vehicle itself was hidden behind their glare.

Margot hurried to her room, took her robe from the closet and put it on, belting it securely around her slim waist as she left the room. She couldn't just sit here shivering with fright. Walking through the dark living room, she carefully opened the front door and leaned outside. She could see the headlights, and the sound of the engine running was much clearer outside, but nobody had come up to the house.

As she looked out, she heard a creaking noise behind her and spun, slamming the front door with her back. The door to the tower, set into the other wall of the entry, had opened slightly, the hinges creaking as it did. She could see an immense blackness lurking in the vast circular room behind the door, gaping like the open mouth of a demon waiting to swallow her up.

Maybe next time.

Margot moved with a giddy feeling of fright to slam the tower door and slip the latch home. Her heart was beating a staccato rhythm within her chest, sending blood flooding to her cheeks and pounding through her head.

Okay, slow down, get a grip. She turned very cautiously, locking and latching the front door. Then she walked to the kitchen and picked up the telephone again. It was still dead. Only then did she realize that the alarm should have gone off when she opened the front door. It hadn't occurred to her at the time that she was breaching her own security, but she had been. And nothing had happened.

The alarm wasn't connected!

She went to the kitchen door, planning to lock it as well, but as she did, she heard a new snatch of song beyond it.

"Margot," someone sang. "Margot, dear Margot..." The rest was lost in the wind.

Shivering against the door, she listened for the song again. A moment later, the wind abated a bit and the singer burst forth.

"Margot, dear Margot, has died in her sleep," went the song.

That was it. The song was sung by a woman—she was certain of that now. An alto or mezzo-soprano, but a woman. Who?

Died in her sleep?

That was enough. Margot hurried to the bedroom and stripped off her robe and nightgown, pulling on her slacks and blouse hastily and then jamming her bare feet into her shoes. She had to get out of here!

She returned to the kitchen and grabbed a steak knife from the drawer. Then, with fear giving her a coldly calm state of mind, she turned the knob of the kitchen door and pulled it open. The rectangle of light from the kitchen stabbed out over the yard to illuminate the sidewalk and the shrubbery along its route but nothing more.

Hoping the diversion would work, she ran quickly around to the living room and twisted the knob of the front door, forgetting the chain latch she'd fastened. The door jerked to the length of the chain and stopped, throwing her off-balance against it for a moment. She closed it again, her calm shattered, and slid the chain off with trembling fingers. Then she threw the door open and ran recklessly into the night.

The wind drove the misting rain into her face as soon as she cleared the safety of the lighthouse tower, but she hurried on, squinting her eyes against the wind. Fearing to go toward the car parked behind her house, she turned to the right to circle the tower at the top of the cliff. There was slightly more than five feet between the tower and the abyss beyond, but it didn't seem nearly that wide in the lightning-punctuated darkness. She kept one hand on the wall of the tower as she continued resolutely around it and finally came in sight of Bellamy's lighted kitchen windows.

There, that was her goal!

She began to run, the leather soles of her shoes slipping on the wet grass, denying her the speed she needed so desperately to get away from the music that had haunted this misting rain.

Turning her head, she saw a human form like a figure cut from black cardboard. It was coming toward her, matching her speed.

Then she slipped, falling in the rain-slicked grass, her knife bounding from her grasp as though someone had snatched it away. She scrambled to her feet again, fighting to breathe against the fear that constricted her throat, and running as she had never run before.

She could hear her pursuer behind her, certainly gaining on her even though she was running, literally, for her life. The light ahead grew, finally making it seem possible to reach her goal.

And then she was there on Edward Bellamy's patio, pounding her fist against his kitchen door.

"Bellamy! Open up!" she cried. She turned her back against the door, staring out over the yard between the houses. There was no one there now. But had they given up? "Bellamy!" she shouted again.

He turned the lock on the door and threw it open to admit her into the safety of his home. She fell into his startled arms, nearly weeping in relief to be safe from the storm and the danger at her heels.

Chapter Eight

"What's wrong?" He held her at arm's length, concern tightening his features as he stared at her in the soft light of his warm kitchen.

"Someone is out there," she gasped. "He was at my house, and followed me."

"Are you certain?" He looked past her through the glass door as he held her more closely.

"Yes, I'm very certain. I saw him outside, wearing one of the masks! And there's a car parked in back of my house with the engine running and the lights on. And they were singing. Oh, God, Bellamy, I couldn't get through on my telephone and the alarm didn't work and I didn't know what else to do, so I just ran."

"Okay, you're safe now. Let's go to my office and get you a drink. Then I'll go over there and check things out."

"No, you shouldn't go over there," she said. "Call the police." She could breathe more easily now, but she wasn't over her shock yet. The singing voice still echoed in her ears. "Who knows what he might do."

"He should be more worried about what *I* might do," Bellamy said resolutely as he led her to the main room and placed her on the couch by the bookcase. "I'll get you something strong to warm you up and then I'll just run over and take a look."

"Do you have a gun?"

"Of course not, but I've got a heavy flashlight in my car. That should do." He spoke calmly and slowly, a grim look haunting his eyes. "Here, drink this down and try not to choke on it. It's very old whiskey and you're going to hate the taste."

She did as she was told, swallowing the drink quickly but still nearly losing her capacity to breath in the harsh aftermath of its passage.

"Damn, you like this stuff, Bellamy?" She cleared her throat, blinking away tears as a new heat began to spread within her stomach.

"I used to have friends," he said. "They liked it."

"Masochists," she proclaimed.

"I'm going to check your house. I'll only be gone a couple minutes. I'm going to leave my house keys here with you. There's a set of switches on my desk to control the locks, so you'll have to let me in when I return."

"Will I know which one to use?" She didn't have to ask why he was leaving his keys inside the house.

"They're labeled. Okay, will you be all right here?"

"Yes, but I still think that you should call the police rather than go over there yourself."

"Probably, but whoever it was is probably gone by now, anyway. We've blown five minutes already. Just relax. The door will lock behind me."

"Be careful," she warned him.

"I'm always careful," he said, letting a small smile come to his expressive lips. "I'll be back before you know it."

He left and a moment later she heard the front door closing behind him. Now she could do nothing but wait and hope that she hadn't sent him into needless danger.

After a moment alone in his house, Margot began to feel better. She began to feel a bit foolish as well. She had burst in on him like a child afraid of a storm. She did have some dignity, didn't she?

No, she reasoned, there had been no room for dignity under the circumstances, and she was glad she'd run as she did. But she was in no condition to go calling.

Her clothing was soaked, and seeing her reflection in the glass over one of his framed book covers, she noted with chagrin that her wet blouse had left no doubt about her lack of an undergarment. The cold fabric that clung like a second skin to her chest left no doubt whatsoever.

Mortification took the rest of her fear away. Luckily, there was a well-worn cardigan draped over the back of a chair by Bellamy's desk. She took the garment and began to slip it on but thought better of it and removed her wet blouse first. The rough weave of the sweater warmed her skin, and the thick wool made her feel less like an exhibitionist.

Margot looked over his desk briefly, locating the row of four switches behind the computer monitor that ran the locks of his house. All were switched on. Beside the keyboard was a sheet of typing paper half filled with couplets apparently meant for the opera.

She walks in a transported light, with skin fair glowing. My concerns fade like night with morning showing.

She scowled slightly. The first was bad and the rest were no better. Presumably, these were rejects. The computer itself was on, but the screen was filled with moving points of light like stars trying to escape the screen. It was a screen-saver program.

All she had to do to see what he had been writing was to move the mouse on its pad near the keyboard. Should she? No, she supposed not, but then she was part of the opera and one of the songs he was working on was hers. It surely wouldn't matter if she looked.

She moved the mouse.

The stars blinked away, replaced by a screen filled with writing. *New neighbor arrived, remodeled, moved in. Life will never be the same.*

That was an odd notation. Below it was written, *Brown hair, hazel eyes, skin of porcelain perfection. Woman of divine humor. Matches her looks. I'm done for.*

Below that was written one word over and over again: *Song, song, song, song.*

He'd been doodling on his computer. It had nothing to do with the opera at all, but with her. She stepped back from the machine, hoping that there would be time before his return for the screen to go back to moving stars. She didn't dare have him know she'd seen this work.

He's lost? Lost because of me?

Margot found herself smiling to think that he was so smitten. The feeling was quite mutual, after all, but she'd been afraid that it might not be. She'd been jealous of a name in a book dedication and worried that he wasn't sincere, while all the time he felt like this about her.

The screen suddenly filled itself with stars again, taking his wonderful words away as though they'd never existed.

Margot carried her glass to the small fridge and found a can of cola inside. She opened it and poured her glass half-full, adding a hint of his whiskey. Her lips turning in a sly smile, she added more whiskey and took her drink back to the desk to glance over the other papers atop it. Nothing else was what she wanted. It was just opera, and the opera was the farthest thing from her mind at the moment.

In the wastebasket beside the desk, however, a stack of wrinkled, darkened papers caught her attention. He'd spilled coffee on them and had thrown them away, and she drew them out now.

I love you, I crave you, can't breathe for this pain of needing you. You taunt me, you bleed me and you damn well don't need me, but still I am tied to this love like a pennant, a flag of surrender, a torn bloodied remnant of what once was a man. The pain of this love, unwanted love, detestable love that loves only to harm, is the one small pleasure I can yet derive from my fantasy union of goddess and fool. I cannot love, yet I love. I cannot feel, but feel too much. Cannot dream without you in my dream, or live without you in my life. I love, believe me. I love you, Marie. I do, Margot, need you. God, make you need me.

Her heart skipped at his typo at the end of the verse.

The bell rang, breaking her reverie, and she dropped the papers back into the trash and flipped the switch marked Intercom.

"Is that you?"

"If you mean, Edward Bellamy, yes, it is I."

Margot flipped the switch for the front door, buttoning up the sweater as she walked away from his desk to meet him.

EDWARD BELLAMY stood outside his door for several minutes before ringing the bell. It was certainly that stupid drunken carpenter who'd scared her so badly. His pickup had still been there when Bellamy drove up, its lights on and engine running, but the man himself wasn't in sight. Edward had gone through the house to make certain that he wasn't inside and found nothing unusual.

He did take time to open the box for the security system and found that it had been tampered with. Gleason could have taken care of that quite easily that afternoon. When he found the carpenter, the man would be damn sorry to have caused Margot even a moment's fright. Killing Jerome Taylor was police business, but harming Margot was personal.

After looking through the rooms, and—foolishly, he felt—checking her progress in the book that lay on her bed, he had gone outside to search the perimeter of the house. As he emerged, he saw the lights of a vehicle sweeping across the yard and ran out just in time to see Gleason's pickup bouncing over the lawn.

He'd watched the lights of the retreating truck until they disappeared around the curve past his own house. He would have loved to have laid his heavy flashlight against the carpenter's skull just then—it was probably best that he hadn't gotten the chance. They knew who to send the cops after now, and that was the important thing.

But it seemed harder to ring his own doorbell than it would have been to beat up the young carpenter. Just the thought of the woman waiting for him inside made him feel weak. He couldn't think of anything but her. The sight of her shivering beneath the inadequate barrier of wet cotton had made his mouth go dry and started a trembling in his fingers that she would surely have noticed if she'd been in any condition to pay attention to such things. Her breasts were perfect, just as perfect as all the rest of her, and her wet shirt had...

No! Stop it. Be a gentleman for once in your life.

But what was a gentleman supposed to do in this circumstance? How was he supposed to behave when a woman who totally dominated his thoughts came to him in the night so vulnerable and so afraid? What was he supposed to do when she looked as she did?

You'll be a gentleman because she is vulnerable and because she is afraid. You can't be anything else now.

He had become a millionaire because he knew the power of fright, and he knew how easily frightened people could be manipulated, tempted away from their better judgment.

But he knew that if he sat too close to her, or if he drank even a drop of the liquor he'd given to her, his own judgment would be lost and his future with her along with it.

He rang the bell feeling nearly as afraid of himself as Margot had been of her visitor. Unfortunately, he couldn't run away from himself. He had learned that much in the last three years.

"DID YOU FIND anything?" Margot hurried to meet him as he entered the room. His hair was wet, and he brushed back the damp curls hanging before his eyes. "I'm not hallucinating, am I?"

"No, you're not. Gleason's pickup was parked outside your house. The little bastard drove off while I was inside." He was glad to see that she'd put on his old sweater. Only now did he realize that he'd neglected to bring any clothing for her to change into. "I guess we know who's behind all of this," he said. "But I sure can't see any connection between him and the opera."

"I thought about that," she said. "It may be a woman we're looking for. That would account for the woman's singing. He could be involved with her."

"Of course," Bellamy exclaimed. "We've been fixated on men, especially since Anne was attacked, but it would make sense that the little creep is hooked up with some irate diva who got the boot. I'll check that with Victor tomorrow."

"What about my telephone and the alarm system?" Margot felt immensely relieved to have any kind of answer just then. She wanted to be rid of this trembling fear, rid of the anxiety the sight of an uncovered window caused her.

"Both of them have been disconnected," Bellamy said. "Gleason probably has a key. He took the security system apart right after they installed it, but he probably left the telephone until he came back tonight."

"He's the only one it could be."

"I'm going to call the sheriff's department right now to report him. He was heading into San Francisco."

"It feels great to finally have an answer," she said with a sigh.

"Well, we don't really have an answer until we know who the woman is," Bellamy said as he dialed. "And you're not going back to your house until they're both behind bars."

"Are you sure I can impose on you by staying?"

"I've got a lovely guest room that nobody ever uses," he told her. "I would be deeply offended if you preferred to be killed over accepting my hospitality."

"All right, you've twisted my arm. I'll stay." She slipped happily into his arms as his call was answered and he began to relate the evening's events to the authorities.

After they'd each finished talking to the police and were assured that a bulletin would go out for the carpenter right away, they set about doing something about her damp clothing. Though she'd removed the shirt, her jeans were still soaked. They went upstairs to find something for her to wear.

He led her to the side door and into the hall connecting his main room to the kitchen. They ascended the open staircase rising in a broad turn against the outer wall, which was nearly completely glass, and entered a room at the top.

It was his bedroom, a large, underfurnished place with only a double bed, a bureau and mirror, and a couple of straight-backed chairs in it. Of course, a grand piano made up for a lack of other furnishings.

"I've got a robe in here someplace," he said, as he crossed to the sliding doors of the closet. "I might have some clothing you could wear, though I really can't say much about women's sizes."

"You keep women's clothing?" Intrigued, Margot joined him at the closet. "Say, what else are you into besides horror writing?"

He frowned slightly. "They were my wife's clothes," he said quickly. "Like I said, I don't know what size she was." He brought out a summer dress, holding the collar to show her the tag.

His wife? "Not my size, I'm afraid," she said. "She must be a tiny woman."

"I guess she was," he said as he busied himself rummaging in the other side of the closet. "It's hard to remember things like that."

"You didn't tell me you were married." Margot took the maroon robe he handed to her. "You don't wear a ring."

"Well, I'm not...that is, not technically married." He walked toward the piano and stared past it through the large window overlooking the sea. "She died," he said, almost as if he were afraid to admit it.

"Oh, I'm sorry." Margot was incapable of finding anything in her suddenly empty mind to say to the man.

"Actually," he said, forced humor coloring his voice, "I do wear a ring." He drew a chain out from the collar of his shirt to display the golden band hanging on it. "I know it seems stupid, but, well, I don't know, I just put in on a chain. You can change in the bathroom behind you."

"Okay, thanks. And then you owe me a piano recital," she said, covering her awkwardness.

"Sure," he said. "But we've got to talk, too. About your caller."

"Not tonight," she said. "I'd rather not dwell on it now that I'm safe and sound."

"You can't ignore it."

"I can for one night, can't I?"

"Yes, I suppose so," he relented. "Say, if you want to shower or anything, feel free. There are towels in the linen cabinet."

"Am I that dirty?" She smiled, feeling more at ease now.

"I don't know." He shrugged. "I've noticed that women like bathing a lot. Besides, it'll give me time to warm up on the piano."

"You're just trying to put off the inevitable," she told him. Then she paused a minute. "Was your wife's name Kay?" she asked him. "I read it in the dedication to your book."

"Yes." He turned and sat at the piano, and Margot closed the bathroom door between them.

She felt that she knew a lot more about him now, probably more than he would have wanted her to know. *Whiteout* made more sense, too, as the anguished lament of a man who felt grief and a certain amount of guilt over the death of his wife. He'd poured his loss into the pages of the book, painting himself as the unthinking protagonist while all of his guilts and fears became the demons that came with the snow. Realizing all of this, Margot was tempted to go out there and give him a big hug just to show that she understood how he had felt.

But she wasn't about to hug him—she didn't really trust herself to touch the man just yet. She'd had just enough of his liquor to lose her judgment.

He was playing the major scales as she removed her wet clothing. Her ankles were muddy, and her feet looked ungainly and pale beneath the spattered ring of grime. Yes, she would take a quick shower after all, rather than be seen like that. She wanted him to see her clean and smelling fresh, so she ran the water and hopped in for a quick scrub followed by a brisk rubbing with the towel that got her blood moving quite nicely.

She took his robe from the hook and slipped into it. The garment swallowed her body, dragging on the floor when she walked and nearly tripping her twice before she gathered it up before her and emerged from the bathroom.

"Where does the audience sit?"

"The audience used to sit on the bed," he said shyly. "You may, if you wish."

"Oh, I don't know if that's proper. This is only our first prowler after all." She sat on the edge of his bed, feeling wicked for being in his bedroom with him, dressed in nothing but his robe. She savored the naughtiness of the feeling. It was especially interesting when she knew that he was probably thinking about the same thing she was just then—his robe, and the single loop of the belt holding it in place.

"I promise I'll stay on my bench," he said, turning to give her a wink. "But if you hear the music stop, watch out."

"Okay, I'll keep an eye on you." She slid up to rest her back against the padded headboard, crossing her bare feet at the ankles where they stuck out of the huge robe. "What's on the program tonight?"

"Chopin, I think. To start with," he said. "And maybe a little Hoagy Carmichael. Any requests?"

"No, play what you enjoy playing."

He began a Chopin étude without further word, his hands moving effortlessly, the broad fingers easily spanning the keys to make playing the piano look as easy as breathing. He closed his eyes while he played, drifting off to his own musical world just as she often did when rehearsing alone.

But who was in that world with him? Was he imagining another audience on the bed? A woman, in a negligee perhaps, for whom this music was a type of foreplay? Was he really playing for Kay once more, using Margot's presence as a stage prop to make it seem more real to him?

He did wear his wedding ring on a chain around his neck, after all. And Kay's clothing was still in the closet.

She pushed those thoughts aside, concentrating instead on the music that filled the room. The piano had a rich mellow sound, and he brought out the best in the instrument as he progressed through the Chopin and then into a rather showy though shortened version of Lizst's *Second Hungarian Rhapsody.* After that came Beethoven's *Moonlight Sonata,* the music lulling her on the soft bed, willing her eyes to slip shut as she drifted on the sensual river of sound.

She didn't notice when the music stopped, for the well-remembered melody continued in her dreaming mind, but she was jolted back to wakefulness when he launched into a rousing rendition of the "The Beer Barrel Polka."

"I wanted to see if you were awake," he called out to her, his left hand rolling out the rhythm while his right danced across the piano, shooting the keys like Chico Marx did in the movies. "I practiced for years to do this," he said. "Cool, huh?"

"Yes, very. The Marx Brothers were always my favorite musicians." She laughed, the mischievous expression on his face bringing her joy. Maybe he *was* playing for her and not the ghost of his wife. Maybe he did enjoy playing for a woman in a man's blue bathrobe.

Then he paused, pursing his lips and thinking of a proper follow-up in the program. "You should sing jazz for a living," he said idly. "You're natural at it. You don't sound like an opera singer at all when you're singing Cole Porter."

"Is that a nasty crack about opera?" she asked, but he didn't reply. He'd already launched into an up-tempo version of Porter's "Night and Day."

That song was followed by Gershwin, Fats Waller, Eubie Blake and more Cole Porter before coming to the promised Hoagy Carmichael.

"I think this is my favorite song," he said, beginning the verse of "Stardust." "Ever since I was a kid, I've liked it. Couldn't tell you why."

The melody, beautifully sad, was answer enough, speaking eloquently of lost love even without the lyrics. And this time, when her eyes began to slip shut, he allowed them to follow their natural course and repeated the song softly.

She felt safe, the music wrapped around her like a blanket, and she dreamed of lying on that bed with him beside her, holding her hand. There was nothing erotic about the dream, for it was a dream of safety that carried her over the threshold into sleep. She awakened only partially when he lifted her from the bed and carried her to the guest room, becoming vaguely aware of their movement and the bulk of his muscles tightening beneath her shoulders and the backs of her legs.

She was safe in bed again, nestled within his sturdy walls and his lovely music as she dreamed of him with her. And the clouds moved away from the moon while she dreamed, giving it a clear and watchful view of the earth once more.

She dreamed that he was kissing her this time, his hands on either side of her face as their lips moved eagerly together. Their bodies pressed against each other and his arms slipped down so that his large, sensitive hands could cup her naked bottom and pull her tightly against his swelling need, drawing her onto him. His arms circled her body, tightened like broad bonds of leather that wouldn't let her go, wouldn't allow her to breathe or escape . . .

And then he dissolved into Tom Gleason, alcohol on his breath and insanity in his eyes as he drew his lips back from hers and sang out, in a woman's sweet alto voice, "Poor Margot, died in bed. Poor Margot died. Died."

She fought against his constricting arms, thrashing and crying out for help until she had kicked her covers off and woke suddenly in a strange moonlit room with a man's bathrobe twisted tightly around her body and the sound of her own startled cry still in the air.

She had no idea where she was at first. Then she remembered. And she remembered who she was with. She felt safe again, tired and safe. Margot stood and threw off the restraining bathrobe.

The door burst open and Bellamy rushed in, crossing nearly to the bed before stopping suddenly in embarrassed confusion.

"I heard you screaming," he explained. "Oh, God, Margot, I'm sorry." But he couldn't take his eyes off her body, naked in the moonlight. "I'll leave you...uh, alone." And yet he was walking toward her, haltingly, waiting for some command to stop.

Any word would have stopped him, but Margot wasn't prepared to say it. Her feet moved of their own will, taking her toward the man who had come to command her heart with total abandon. The moonlight glimmered off his muscular chest, accenting the sensuous curves of his reaching arms, enticing her further as she rushed to meet him, throwing herself into those arms and accepting those broad hands upon her as though her life depended upon their touch.

She'd never wanted anyone as she wanted this man. Her hands were on the waistband of his pajamas and tearing them down even as they first kissed. His welcome pressure against her leg drove them both on, their lips moving hungrily on each other as they stumbled back toward the bed. They fell upon it and into a fusion of burning need that rose to a crescendo, their movements providing a symphony of glorious sensations. The silken feeling of his body slipping between her clutching legs, hands grasping her firmly, possessively, lips devouring her lips, brought Margot to the edge of a world that began in the center of her womanhood and seemed to extend beyond all measure until it exploded around them, leaving them shaken and wrapped in each other's arms for a brief moment until they rolled and joined, wordlessly, again.

This time, warm in her lover's arms, she slept without dreaming as the guardian moon washed in through the window. Its light seemed especially gentle and kind tonight.

The moonlight shone on the placid waters of the Pacific Ocean, sparkling over the small ripples as the tide washed to shore. It was reflected from the puddled water on the lawns and from the windows of the two houses on the cliff. And the moonlight was reflected catlike by the eyes of the lone man standing at the base of the lighthouse tower, watching Bellamy's darkened house.

Only the moon heard his song.

Chapter Nine

The morning sun glowed softly through the tall window, a light mist mellowing its light to a golden color as it warmed the guest room and slowly brought Margot back from the land of her dreams. She was alone in the bed, but the pillow beside her still bore the indentation of Bellamy's head, and she smoothed her hand over it lovingly. She didn't want to move for fear that this wonderful feeling would be lost.

When she did move, it was to slip her legs over the edge of the bed and sit, shaking her long hair back languorously as she stretched her muscled back to wakefulness. Then she stood, looking around the tastefully furnished room in approval. The carpet was plush, the furnishings colored in warm, sedate tones. The room made her feel welcome.

The robe she'd been wearing was on the floor by the bed, and she picked it up as she walked to the door that should, if she had her bearings, be a guest bath.

The bathroom was large and warm, with towels laid out and waiting, so she treated herself to a shower. Then, her hair combed back and bound with an elastic band from the vanity drawer, she padded downstairs barefoot in Bellamy's large robe.

He was already at his keyboard.

"Good morning," she said as she entered the room.

"A very good morning," he agreed. He swiveled his chair around to face her, smiling as he stretched his arms up and back to intertwine his fingers behind his head. "I was right about you," he said.

"How so?" Margot walked over and rested her hip against the edge of his desk, folding her hands together before her as she looked at the man in whose home she'd just passed so peaceful a night.

"You wake up early and in a good mood," he said. "I thought so."

"And why were you thinking that?"

"Idle speculation. I have little else to occupy my time than wonder about the sleeping habits of neighbors."

"Now your knowledge is a bit more complete," she replied.

"Oh, yes." He nodded, bringing his hands down again to rest them on his knees. "I...that is, I wanted to tell you that last night was wonderful."

"Absolutely wonderful," she said.

"But, I don't want you to get the wrong impression," Bellamy said quickly, then paused as though to find the right words.

Margot's heart sank under the leaden certainty that he was going to break her heart.

"What kind of impression do you think I have?" she asked him carefully.

"I don't know." He frowned, standing. "I just wanted to be clear. I think you're wonderful—perfect, really. But I don't want to rush anything. Last night didn't turn out the way I expected. I hadn't planned to make love with you."

"And I did?" she asked. "Do you think I came here planning that?"

"No," he said quickly. "No, certainly not. I just didn't want you to think that I planned to take advantage of you. I'm saying this awkwardly, but I just don't want to blow it. I want the two of us to work."

Margot smiled then, shaking her head. "I thought you were going to tell me something else," she said. "You had me worried."

"Oh, no, I'm sorry." He came to her and took her into his arms. "On paper, I have a chance to edit my words, but in person I'm stuck with a rough draft. I just don't want to repeat old mistakes and end up losing you."

"You won't lose me."

"Oh, I hope not," he said on a sigh. "Of course, we also have to keep you alive." He kissed her cheek and stood back, trailing his hands over her shoulders before pulling them away. "I called the police this morning, but they haven't found Gleason yet."

"They'll get him."

"Oh, I'm sure they will. But we should be careful until they do." He smiled. "Meanwhile, I believe it's time for breakfast. Now let me guess—you're a wheat toast and fruit person in the morning. Right?"

"Close enough. Is that something else you've speculated about?"

"A bit, though not as much as other things," he said, offering her his arm. "I would like to invite you to the kitchen for the morning meal."

"I accept your invitation gladly." She took his arm, walking at his side across the room. "I should ask about my clothing, however. I imagine my place is overrun by painters by now, so I can hardly return in your robe."

"Your shirt and jeans are in the dryer," he told her. "I took the liberty of tossing them in with my things. I hope you don't mind."

"Not at all. I certainly don't object to a gentleman taking liberties."

"Yes, but we already know that I'm no gentleman," he said as they left the room.

AFTER BREAKFAST, they walked slowly along the road between Bellamy's house and hers, two people lost in conversation on a two-lane country road. Bellamy pledged to stay at her side until the matter was closed, ignoring her halfhearted pleas that she could take care of herself.

"Humor me," he said. "And give me this excuse to hang around with you. Okay?"

"Okay," she told him. "But what about after they've caught him? What will your excuse be then?"

"I hope I won't need one."

Margot was glad to have gained his protection. Even though they masked their fear with jokes, she was truly frightened by the prospect of being caught alone as Anne had been. The man who had called her certainly intended to do more than bruise her throat.

They let the matter rest as they walked to her house, speaking of more pleasant things.

"We built here nearly six years ago," Bellamy said. "Charlie Adamson, the lightkeeper, was here then, though the light was already decommissioned."

"Did you ever see the light on?"

"Charlie used to run it a couple times a year, the Fourth of July and Christmas. I suppose he missed the darn thing after so long, but he probably only turned it on because Uncle Sam was still paying the electricity on the joint."

"It must have been quite a sight when the light was running." Bundled into Bellamy's woolen pea coat, Margot felt a certain kinship with the old sailors and their lighthouse on the cliff. The chill wind blowing up from the sea that morning and the smell of rain and ocean had put her in a mood of nostalgia for an era she had never seen. "It would be so romantic on a foggy night to see that light sweeping through the mist."

"You could always go up and turn it on," he suggested. "Find out for yourself."

"Do you think so? I assumed that it no longer worked."

"It worked two years ago. Might need a bit of grease for the gears, but the light should be fine. You could run it for your housewarming," he suggested. "That way your guests know how to find you."

"Is that legal?"

"Sure. It's your light now. You paid enough for it."

"I'll do that. Though I didn't know I was having a party."

"You don't understand the concept of a housewarming," he said, stopping at the end of her driveway and watching the sea beyond the tower. "You have to fill the house with laughter and good thoughts to banish any bad spirits that may linger from the past lives that were spent there. Of course, with the crowd you've got at the opera, who knows what kind of karma you'd install in place of the old."

Margot laughed. The idea of Daniel Pressman being good for the spirit of any home amused her.

"But you're not serious, are you? You made that up."

"Human beings thrive on superstition. Besides, it's as good an excuse for a party as any other."

"That's true. I guess I'll have to bow to superstition on that one. But if anyone spills anything on my new carpeting, it's not going to be good for the house's spirit."

"Oh, I don't know," he said, grinning down at her. "Blood sacrifices are traditional for new ventures, too."

They continued along the driveway to her home, entering through the kitchen door. The smell of paint was overpowering.

Bellamy wrinkled his nose, scowling. "It smells like you've got one more reason to be my guest for another night."

"They're using oil paint," she explained. "I wanted it to last."

"These toxic fumes will probably last as long as the paint."

They walked into the living room. Two young men were busy rolling a sea green paint onto the walls while another was busy taping around the windows to do the woodwork.

"You're right," she agreed. "I can't sing if my nose and throat have swelled shut from the fumes."

"There's probably a clause about that in your contract."

"They are doing their job with a vengeance, aren't they?"

In fact, there were painters busy upstairs in her sitting room and bedroom as well. By the time the day was through, the house would have its first coat of interior paint throughout. A second coat would go on tomorrow. She had paid a premium for rapid completion, and she was surely getting her money's worth.

"This is a great house," he said after they'd completed their tour. "Have you been up the tower yet?"

"Once, with the realtor. Nothing but dust up there."

"Show me. I've never been at the top."

"Okay," she said, leading him to the entrance by the front door. "But I'm afraid I've stored my things at the bottom of the stairs. It might be a climb to get through them."

It didn't take too great an effort to pass her stored things, for, as she realized now, she didn't really have very much to get past. A few boxes contained clothing, while some other boxes were books and only two boxes held mementos, some from childhood, some from high school. Bellamy picked up something from the top of an open carton near the spiral iron stairs that circled the outer wall of the tower.

"You still play with dolls, Margot?" he asked, holding her old Raggedy Ann tenderly in one hand.

"My mother sent a box of things out when I told her I was buying a place," Margot explained. She took the doll, looking lovingly at the worn face and the frayed cloth body of her oldest friend. "I had nearly forgotten her, but once upon a time we were inseparable."

"Looks like she was well loved."

"Loved nearly to death, from the looks of her," Margot said. She put the doll down, but then thought better of it and picked it up again, saying, "Now that we're back together, I really shouldn't make her lie in a box."

"No, that's no way to treat an old friend."

They climbed the stairs quickly. Though both were in good condition, they were winded when they stepped up through the trapdoor into the circular glass-walled room at the top of the tower.

The light was a large lens, like a massive flashlight mounted atop a platform connected to the large cogs and gears of the rotation apparatus below. The room was warm from the sunlight flooding in from every direction, and it smelled of dust and old grease on the gears. There was nothing else up there but a metal electrical box on the wall near the head of the stairs.

"Is that the switch?" Margot shifted the doll from one hand to the other and pointed at the lever extending from one side of the box.

"Must be. I believe there's a time mechanism downstairs someplace," he said. "Charlie mentioned its needing repairs once."

"Were you good friends with this Charlie?"

"Not really, but we were both alone out here, so we had a beer now and again. He was a widower." Bellamy looked through the dirty glass at the land around them. "They raised three sons here. I would guess that the Interior Department's decision to sell the light gave him an out to move in with one of them."

"How so?"

"His kids had asked him to do it since his wife died, but he was too independent. Didn't want to be a bother and didn't think he needed anyone's help with anything. I suspect that he found independence a bit lonely. He cleared out pretty quickly once word came down about the sale."

"The realtor said there was still food in the refrigerator when she came to check it out."

"There you go," he mused. "People can only be alone for so long."

Bellamy walked to the glass door opening out toward the south. The latch was stiff, its lock rusted a bit by the sea air, but he leaned his weight into it and it gave way, letting the door swing haltingly outward on its rusty hinges.

Cool air flooded through the door, dispersing the greenhouse heat like a shower of cold water. Margot held her coat closed with one hand as she joined him on the balcony that circled the glass lamp housing. The wind was quite brisk.

"If you took the light out, you'd have a nice little solarium up here. A little hideaway where you can see trouble coming."

"You expect trouble?" she asked. She rested her hand lightly on the railing that progressed around the tower walk. Her attention was focused on the man before her, noting how he had become more somber after their climb.

"Not really," he said, walking along the seaward side of the tower and stopping to look back at her. "But it usually shows up. Maybe you haven't had that problem. You've done very well so far."

"As have you."

"Well, I've been successful, if that's what you mean. But things balance out." He walked back toward her, looking at her seriously, the wind blowing his hair back wildly while his icy blue eyes regarded her with a measure of concern. His lips, bracketed by thoughtful creases, were firm and unsmiling up here where the wind blew unchecked from the sea. "You always pay for what you get."

"But that's only fair," Margot said. "You can't expect to get something for nothing." She traced one finger over the top of the railing.

"I don't." He scowled, leaning his broad shoulder against the glass beside the door. "But a man expects that his hard work is the payment. He doesn't know about the many other costs involved in success until the bills come due."

He turned to lean his back against the glass and look out over the sea, his hands in the pockets of the denim jacket he'd worn. A wistful expression overcame his face just then, a look that appeared to Margot like regret.

She went to him, placing one hand softly on his upper arm as she looked up into his eyes. She wanted to say something to dispel the look in his eyes, but wasn't sure of the cause or the cure.

"Charlie Adamson used to come up here in the afternoons to look over the sea," he said quickly, as though wanting to cut off any possible words she might offer. "I'd see him up here, unmoving, for hours. Now he's in Phoenix, I think. I wonder if he spends his afternoons looking out over the desert like he did at the sea. And I wonder if he ever sees anything."

"What is there to see?" She glanced at the ocean, following his gaze to the misty horizon. "There's nothing there."

"No, there isn't." He smiled then, lifting one hand to rub his cheek idly. "And maybe that's what we want to see. Nothing. No matter what we're looking for, I don't think we really want to see anything there."

"The payment?" she asked. "You don't want to see it coming?"

"Yes, that's it. We expect the bill to come due, but we sure as hell don't want to get it. I think that maybe your drunken carpenter last night was part of your payment."

"How so?"

"You're famous, you know. You've even begun moving into the mainstream, into popular music. You're bound to attract unwanted attention."

"I've already got that in the opera."

"But operagoers appreciate restraint, otherwise they wouldn't be opera buffs. Popular music has always had a radical element among its fans."

"You sound like my agent," she said. "Warning me against becoming too public."

"Your agent's probably right." Bellamy reached toward her then, almost but not quite touching her with his left hand before letting it drop to his side. "Performers have been killed by their fans, you know. And the person who appears most normal is quite often anything but."

"You read too many scary stories." She laughed, trying to shrug off the chill that his words had put into her heart. "Young Mr. Gleason is not a fan."

"He may not be the man we want, either."

"Please, Bellamy, I thought we had that much established," she exclaimed.

"I hope we do," he said. "But what if we don't? What if he's just some drunken carpenter who wants to protect you from the boogeyman?"

"Then who could it be?"

"Maybe it is just one man. No woman."

"I'm sure it was a woman singing, Bellamy. The funny thing was that she knew the music from the opera. She knew my songs."

"Which lyrics?" he asked, folding his arms before him.

"Lyrics? She . . . wait, they were the new ones!" Margot suddenly felt as though reality had shifted below her. Nobody could have known the new lyrics to her aria, not when she'd only known them since that morning herself. "They were *your* words, Bellamy," she whispered, grasping the railing beside her and leaning on it. "How could he have known?"

Reality did shift then. The railing in her hand snapped off, and her hand, still holding the doll and the two-foot bar of metal, flew out, leaving nothing but the wind to support her weight. With a sudden gasp, Margot tried to shift back, jerking her body forward in vain as her left foot slipped past the edge of the walkway.

The world was suddenly a swirling panorama of sea and sky and the dark rocks below, with nowhere at all to find footing.

Bellamy leaped forward, his long arm shooting out just as she began to fall and catching the lapel of her coat. Her weight brought his chest hard against the railing that remained, but it held. With a convulsive heave backward, he pulled her to him, and they both fell gasping against the glass wall of the tower.

Neither of them spoke for a moment but stood holding each other tightly, her cheek pressed against the rough texture of his jacket as he held her head to him. They were both trembling, frightened and suddenly very aware of the life that had nearly been snatched away.

"I guess I'll have to do a few more structural repairs than I had thought," she said at last.

Bellamy didn't say anything but just laughed, stroking her hair with one hand while holding her firmly with the other.

After they had caught their breaths, they caught their sense of propriety as well and parted carefully. The wind seemed to have grown to a gale force and the platform beneath her feet suddenly appeared riddled with decay, even though it was just as sturdy as it had been a moment before. Margot wanted to get down from this precipice.

But she couldn't leave without taking one look at the broken railing and the rocks below it. Like a person who had witnessed a car wreck, she found it fascinating in retrospect.

"Careful," Bellamy warned, stepping up beside her as she looked over the edge.

"I'm not about to lean on it," Margot assured him.

The sea rolled in foamy waves against the rocks at the base of the cliff. It was so far down that the sound of the sea was overtaken by the sound of the wind around them. The rocks seemed harmless and unreal from up here, like a stage set rather than the deadly peril they were.

"Oh, my God," Margot gasped. She did lean on the railing then, steadying her downward gaze. "Bellamy, look."

Below her, moving slightly with the action of each wave, a man's body lay twisted on the wet rocks. And, though she couldn't see his face from this distance, he looked shockingly familiar.

"It's the carpenter," she said when Bellamy came to her side. "It's Tom Gleason."

Chapter Ten

"The kid didn't show up for work yesterday at all. I don't have any idea where he was." Ralph Dorn, the contractor Margot had hired for her remodeling, spoke authoritatively when the sheriff's deputy questioned him. He talked with his cigarette still in his mouth, the smoking cylinder bobbing in rhythm with his words. "All I can really tell you is that he was a pretty good worker. Not the best, you know, but good. Always early on site, too."

Margot sat rather numbly on a chair at the food bar separating her kitchen from the dining room and listened to a police officer asking Dorn questions. Bellamy had gone out to check on the progress the police on the Coast Guard launch were making at getting the body off the rocks, leaving her momentarily alone with the two men.

The officer, a thirtyish man with blond hair and dark eyes, voiced his questions in the offhand manner of someone bored with his job. Dorn, a heavyset man in his fifties, spoke much more forcefully than the officer, overshadowing the official nature of the younger man's work with his gruff impatience. Time was money to Ralph Dorn, and this business was costing him time.

Margot hadn't talked to the officer yet. The contractor had arrived with his bill while they were waiting for the police to come and so was there when the deputy did get there. Margot wondered if the man would bill her for his time answering questions.

"Are you done with me or what?" he asked. "I've got another job just starting up and most of my guys can't be trusted to pick up a hammer if I'm not on top of them."

"Sure, go on," Deputy Albert Simmons told the big man. "Thank you for your time." He was already turning away, bringing his notebook and his halfhearted questions over to Margot as he spoke.

"So, you say that the man was here last night?" Deputy Simmons softened his tone somewhat, but didn't seem any more interested in her story than he was in the painting that was still going on around them.

"Yes, at least his pickup was here. I never actually saw him well enough to be certain of his identity."

"He was harassing you?"

"Doing his best, yes."

"How?"

"Looking in the windows and such. And someone was singing. Did anyone find a mask and opera cape out there?"

"No, we didn't find anything like that. Do you think this Gleason is connected to the events at the opera house?"

"Come on, do you guys think that someone would be harassing her at home coincidentally to the stuff going on in the city?" Bellamy stepped into the house then and approached the two in the kitchen. "Of course it's related."

"It would seem that way," the officer said, "but it never pays to make assumptions. Of course, I would assume that he lost his footing on the wet grass," the officer said. "Unless there was someone else out there."

"I didn't see anyone else," Margot said, unwilling to complicate matters with speculation on the woman who was singing in the fog.

"So what did you do with Gleason's vehicle?"

"His what? His truck?" Margot was suddenly struck by the singular fact that Gleason's pickup *had* been gone this morning, and with him lying on the rocks below her house, there was no way that it *could* have been gone. "I—I don't know what happened to his pickup," she told the deputy. "It should be here."

"No, he drove away in it last night," Bellamy said. "While I was inside checking the house, he drove off."

"And yet he came back without his vehicle and fell off the cliff?" The officer's voice gained an edge. Apparently he was a bit more interested in the case now.

"Yes."

"Does that make sense to either of you?" the officer asked.

"No," Margot admitted, "it doesn't make any sense at all."

"Yet that seems to be what happened," Bellamy said.

"I'm not going to make any such assumptions, and I suggest that you people don't either. So, is there anything else you can think of? Either of you?"

"No," Margot said. "There isn't really anything that I can add to what I've already said."

"Neither can I," Bellamy said. "But it's fairly clear what happened, I think. No matter why he was here or why he moved his truck, the fact is that he got too close to the edge of the cliff and slipped off. Right?"

"Probably," the deputy said. "That railing up there was cut, you know. Somebody used a hacksaw to cut most of the way through."

"I thought so," Bellamy said. "It seemed odd that it broke on both sides like that."

"That's probably what he was doing the other night," Margot said.

"He was awfully drunk then, Margot," Bellamy said. "Unless he was just faking it so I'd go away."

"It doesn't really matter now, though," the deputy said. "So what connection does this carpenter have with your opera?"

"None," Margot said. "But there must have been something."

"Either that or he was innocent and there's still someone else trying to get you. We'll keep up our patrol until we can be sure. Thank you for your help." He closed his notebook and picked up his hat from the serving bar and placed it squarely on his head. "Goodbye now," he told them. And then he walked out of the door.

"He's right, you know," Bellamy said.

"Yes, I know," she admitted. "Gleason couldn't be the same man who attacked Anne. He was working when that happened."

"That could have been him, but probably not. He was probably out here for just the reason he told me," Bellamy said. "I suppose he had a crush on you and came out to make sure you were safe."

"Oh, God, Bellamy, this is so horrible," Margot said. "I can't believe something like this has happened."

"The guy was wandering around your yard in the dark in the middle of a rainstorm," Bellamy said. "And probably drunk, too. He slipped."

"Yes, but that doesn't make it any less horrible." Margot felt ill just thinking about the fall he had taken, wondering if he'd been alive down there—for hours, perhaps—before finally dying. It was too much to think about. She rubbed her forehead firmly with both hands, closing her eyes with a sigh.

"Are you all right?"

"I've got a headache."

"Why don't you pack some things and come over to my place?" he said. "You've had a bad morning, and your house is full of paint fumes, not to mention strange men in painting coveralls. You won't get much rest here."

"But I've got to go in to work."

"Why? You're a big star, aren't you? Take a day off."

"I can't do that," she scoffed. "We've only got three weeks."

"It's up to you, of course, but you can't do much until you learn the new lyrics. They're here, not in the city."

"You finished?"

"Yes, I wrote the aria last night." He couldn't stop a smile from coming to his face when he thought of the song he'd written for her.

"Can I see it?" The news almost served to lessen Margot's depression over Tom Gleason. "Will you play it for me?"

"I didn't say I could play the music," he cautioned, "only that I finished the lyrics."

"You're too modest, Bellamy. You can play it."

"I guess the only way you'll find out if I can or not is to pack a bag and come over."

"Do you have some ulterior motive in getting me over there?" She stood, eyeing the man with a wicked smile.

"I think keeping you alive is motive enough."

"Maybe, but there are other motives I'd like better," she teased.

As she went to pack some clothing, the Coast Guard motor launch was just pulling away from the base of the cliff, its plastic-wrapped burden safely gathered from the rocks. They moved out to the larger Coast Guard ship that awaited them and then headed to San Francisco.

A mile south, in the thick of the Federal Wildlife Preserve, a man watched their progress with a pair of binoculars. After the boat had pulled away, he brought the lenses down from his eyes and walked past the pickup truck concealed in the foliage to the gray Mercedes that was idling on the narrow rutted roadway.

Once in his car, he turned up the volume of the receiver that was running on the passenger seat. "I had better call and tell them I'll be in later," Margot was saying. "Call from my place," Bellamy said, his voice crackling slightly over the small speaker.

Good, I'll have time to get there before her, he thought, slipping the car into gear.

"Say, I found your friend," Bellamy was saying as the foreign car drove south to the other entrance of the preserve.

"What?" Margot came out with her overnight case in one hand and Bellamy's book in the other.

"Raggedy Ann." He held the doll out to her. "She's a little damp but otherwise in sound condition."

"Oh, I forgot about her!" Margot put her case down and took the doll from him, examining the fabric carefully.

"She's had a new experience," he said, picking her bag up.

"I might have lost her for good," Margot said, feeling suddenly sad again.

It seemed appropriate that the doll had taken the fall in her place. But after so long a time without a thought for her old best friend, it seemed incredibly cruel to have dropped her. Such was the unconditional love that passed between a child and her plaything.

THE WEATHER had changed overnight, the sky clearing to a magnificent azure shade as though last night's storm had marked the end of something, and the dawn a new beginning.

Margot felt that she knew Bellamy better now because of the unhesitating way he offered her his home when she needed its refuge. He hadn't resorted to any male posturing or exaggerated protectiveness when he secured her house for her, but had simply taken care of the task and moved on from there. He didn't ask awkward questions or give too much unwanted advice, yet she could tell that he was keenly interested in her well-being.

Edward Bellamy was not a demonstrative man, but one who simply stood solidly by, his friendship ready when needed.

But there was something behind his wit and somewhat sarcastic manner that bespoke great pain. He kept himself reserved, hidden away. What part of himself that did come out was communicated through his writing; his book and the wonderful lyrics he'd written showed that. But that was a one-way communication, not a dialogue. Margot wanted to find a way through to a dialogue.

And she hoped that what happened between them last night was only the beginning for them.

He drove her into town, offering the excuse that he had to meet with Daniel Pressman, anyway. She had accepted the ride because their being together simply felt natural. She enjoyed his company even if they didn't speak.

Margot had been raised to be self-sufficient, to follow her own course in life and accept the consequences. She had learned early to take objective stock of her own capabilities and act accordingly, and so had never been at a loss when she was on her own. Now, however, she felt a certain emptiness at the thought of being alone. It wasn't loneliness, either, but a much more disturbing feeling—incompleteness.

The feeling had come upon her so quickly that she hadn't had time to subject it to her usual analysis, but had simply accepted it as a fact. She needed him.

She had a clue why he still had his wife's clothing in his closet and why he wore his wedding ring on a chain around his neck. He had loved Kay and felt incomplete without her. And, though he may not be lonely and may be able to function without her, somewhere deep inside, it felt as though a piece of his mind had been torn out with her death.

This morning, on the light tower, he had been talking about looking for the bill coming due. He had begun to open up, obviously struggling to find the words to explain his feelings without quite admitting to them. He spoke like a man who had paid the bill when it càme. And spoke like a man who was unwilling to pay again.

Margot had never had to struggle for her goals. Her voice had opened doors for her. Perhaps her bill had merely been defrayed. Or, more possibly, she hadn't been aware of the payments. Her life of motion and solitude might be the payment, something which she wouldn't be aware of until later when she looked back in regret on all the chances lost over the years.

Meeting Edward Bellamy had certainly caused her to look at her life now. And, now that she felt this communion with him, she knew she could never return to the life she had lived without a daily sense of regret. That would be a steep payment indeed for her success.

Once they reached the opera house, Margot went to wardrobe while Bellamy was taken away by the directors of the company for a conference that he was clearly unwilling to attend. He gave the music to Margot when they parted, saying, "Give this to Grimaldi. I can't trust these guys not to lose it."

Avery Lister laughed heartily at that comment, though Margot knew that Bellamy had been quite serious about it. His opinion of opera itself was obviously higher than his opinion of opera managers.

Victor Grimaldi wasn't in his office or the rehearsal hall, so Margot went in search of Pamela Laurie instead, finding her seated at her sewing machine.

The woman scowled up at her when she entered, and removed several pins from her mouth. "So, the queen finally arrives," she said. "How the hell do you expect me to finish anything without your bod to stuff into it? You people think I'm a miracle worker."

"I'm sorry, but there was a man killed at my house this morning." Margot laid the music on the table, wishing that she was already through with her fitting.

"Gee, too bad," Pamela said, "but life goes on, doesn't it? Here, put this on. And if you've gained an ounce anywhere, I'll cut it off with my shears."

Margot took the outfit, an exaggerated and highly stylized waitress uniform for her first act, and went behind the screen to change.

"What about the red dress?" Margot asked. "Did Daniel talk to you about changing it?"

"I told him where to stick his changes, honey. The dress is finished and I've got no time to bother with finished work."

"Tell me something, Pam," she said as she disrobed. "Why are you so angry?"

"Me? Angry? The egos around this joint would piss off Mother Teresa, dear, or hadn't you noticed?"

"Sure, but why let them get to you?"

"What are you, a Girl Scout?" Pamela lit a cigarette and happily drew in a lungful of smoke. "Of course, you're on top of the heap, aren't you? It's easy for you to ignore those toads."

"But you're back here away from them most of the time. You should be able to ignore them, too."

"Tucked away in the bowels of the musical machine," Pamela said, laughing. "That's me. I've been digested."

Margot stepped out from behind the screen, adjusting the costume. "You should give them a chance."

"I did once," Pamela mused. "It was a mistake. A big mistake."

"Really? What happened?"

"You don't want to know. Besides, he went off to become rich and famous and I'm still here with pins in my mouth."

"I've never met anyone so determined to be depressed," Margot commented. "You should try to lighten up."

"Don't mind me, honey. Once I've had my smoke break, I'm an entirely different woman. Okay, let's take a look at you. Damn! You *lost* weight!" She stubbed out her cigarette and tugged at the fabric at Margot's hip. "Go eat something," she snarled. "I'm not taking the damn thing in!"

BY THE TIME Margot was finished trying on her reconstructed costumes, she felt as though she had already put in a full day. Connie Dwight's excitement took a bit of that feeling away, however, when they met in the hall outside Victor's practice studio.

"This is great!" the ebullient blonde proclaimed, taking Margot's hands into hers. "I've risen to such a position of respect since I got a solo that I've even got Pam mad at me. Victor won't rehearse with me anymore, either. He says there are others who need help and he doesn't have time to waste on people who have their parts down pat.''

"I take it that you like being a star," Margot said.

"Just great! But what about you? I hear that you and a certain author you'd never heard of have hit it off pretty well. Have you guys gotten to *know* each other yet?" she asked with a broad wink.

"You have a filthy mind." Margot joined her laughter, hugging her friend to her as much in an effort to cover her sudden blushing as in mirth. "And it's none of your business, anyway."

"Like hell. I always spilled the beans."

"Maybe you did, but I never asked."

"Okay, so you've got more class than I do, but that's no reason to keep secrets."

"Well, I did spend the night at his house last night," Margot said, letting her words linger teasingly.

"Yes, yes?"

"Yes, nothing. Sorry dear, but I've got to find Victor. You'll have to keep your libido on hold for now," she said as she opened the door. "I'll see you later."

"Ah, Margot!" Victor exclaimed, crossing from his piano to meet her. "I understand that you have something for me."

"Yes, Edward told me to give you this." She handed him the score Bellamy had entrusted to her. "It's the last aria. That's all of it now, isn't it?"

"Yes, all of it is repaired." He hurried back to the piano, studying the pages as he went. "Come, we shall sing through some of... wait, he's..." Victor stopped speaking and sat at the piano and spread the music out before him. Margot could see several places in the music where additional notations had been made, and it was at these passages that Victor was squinting with deep concentration.

He sat back, placed his hands on the keyboard and played the music once. Then he played it again, but with subtle differences.

"Yes," he said then, flipping the pages in search of other changes but finding none. "Yes, he may be right." Then he laughed, turning to look up at Margot. "Leave it to him to change my music to suit his words. The boy was never short of ego."

"He changed the music?"

"Suggested changes," Victor said. "But you see how he's shortened the lyric from the former line. We have the choice of adding beats to the words to stretch them or cut music to fit the words. He has always preferred the succinct to the copious."

"And you'll let him do that?"

"I don't know if I'll let him or not," Victor said. "I'll study the changes for myself. He's got a good head for music."

"Is that why you had wanted him to collaborate with you on the show?"

"Certainly, but mostly because he has a better head for words." He laughed again, shaking his head. "He was my student at Juliard years ago."

"Music school? He didn't tell me that."

"Oh, I'm sure he didn't. He was studying composition. Gifted, perhaps, but not profoundly so. It was in performance that he shone. Those hands, such a range in those hands."

"But he's not in music now? Why not, if he was so talented?"

"Oh, his talent is better served with words, I think," the man said, nodding his head. "His music, too, perhaps. Have you read his work?"

"Half of one book."

"Well, then maybe you, too, can see that he writes in musical form. Each book is a work of music, and the words keep to a rhythm constant with the piece he is playing. That one called *Storm Garden* was a waltz. He admitted as much to me when I asked. You can feel the movement of the music in the words, almost hear it."

"What about *Whiteout*?"

"Oh, that one." Victor scowled. "That is a strange sort of opera, I think. A grand solo performance. If he had written it after his wife died, it would perhaps have been a dirge. But, no, I don't think he would have written it after."

"I thought he had. I just assumed—that he'd written it about her death."

"No, no, it was after she left him. A plea, yes, a confession, that is what it is. Written by a man alone with his soul and not liking the company."

"Why did she leave him?" Margot pulled a folding chair up beside the bench.

"I shouldn't gossip like a pigeon on the stoop," he said. "But, tell me, is it true that you and Edward have become friends? The talk is thick around here."

"Yes, it's true, Victor. He's not very open, though."

"Never was. That's not a worry, it means nothing."

"What about his wife?" Margot had never liked gossip, but on this subject her interest was too keen to hold back.

"Between you and me, Kay was not for him. She was a flashy woman, a gadabout, and she spent money as you and I might breathe. Edward fell in love with her energy,

I think. She brought him out of himself, made him think that things were possible. In the end, though, she could never accept that he was not the same as she. He didn't run to parties or jet off to premieres, even though he had ample opportunity. The house was the last straw for Kay. She didn't like the seclusion, couldn't take being alone with her thoughts. And then, Edward is not so easy a person to live with, either. Not if you dislike silence.''

''You know quite a bit about them.''

''Yes, I was a frequent guest at the house before she left. Not so much after. He hasn't done much entertaining since that time—he has spent as much time as possible in Europe, actually. I don't think he would have come back for this if I hadn't all but gotten on my knees for his help.'' Victor laughed once more, grinning wickedly. ''The bastards were frantic to rescue their company after they realized what a mess they had on their hands. Even before Taylor had his unfortunate accident, they were trying to get Edward back. They thought they could play on our friendship to get an artist to take the place of a hack.''

''But he did come,'' Margot said.

''Of course, because I called and did my own begging. What choice did we have after Jerome's death? But the company paid a high price for the service, you see. He's obtained a piece of the box office for the right to put his name on the marquee. It was his name as much his writing that they wanted, after all, so it was right that they pay well for it.''

''This all sounds rather Machiavellian,'' Margot commented. ''It doesn't sound like anyone was interested in putting on an opera, only making a deal.''

''Yes, just like Hollywood.''

''I didn't know what I was walking into when I came here,'' Margot commented.

"You were walking into fate, my dear," he said. "This part will cement your reputation—especially now, with Edward's lyrics." He turned back to the pages on the piano. "Yes, I think you have inspired him. He's made Marie into a very contemporary heroine, a woman without equal in the end, I think. I think the true inspiration shows in Trierweiller's solo, however, but that makes sense. Edward always writes best in the first person."

Margot felt a sudden blush rise to her cheeks at his words. She had heard the tenor's love song, and, if it was in any way autobiographical, Bellamy had managed to answer all of her questions about their relationship. In fact, he had communicated his feelings better than he might have done in person.

"Oh, I have embarrassed you." Victor laughed, slapping his knee and then turning to the piano to play a triumphal major chord. "You will, of course, invite me to the wedding?"

"Goodness, Victor, I..." She cleared her throat, struggling to find another subject to talk about.

"Victor, can you think of anyone who wouldn't want this opera produced?"

"Wouldn't? Goodness no, dear. I can think of many people who might want to burn the theater to the ground or kill Daniel or myself, but none who might have a grudge against this piece."

"Who might want to burn the theater then?"

"Any number of people who have been cast out of the troupe," Victor said. "Many singers have gone on to do well in other areas of performance, and they occasionally stop by to let us know they didn't need us after all. I think their need for revenge is satisfied on those visits. Martin Andrews was one of those."

"The mimic?"

"Yes, he was always gifted at imitation if nothing else. But he is a millionaire now and hardly one to need revenge."

"Would anybody have keys to the place? And would any of them know their way around well enough to get around unseen?"

"I don't know such details," he said, shrugging. "Of course Neil and—"

Victor's words were cut off by a sudden shout from the hall. They hurried to the door and discovered people running outside.

"Are we on fire?" Victor asked.

"No, they're headed back, not out," Margot said. "Come on."

They joined the flow moving back toward the work spaces behind the stage, and down to where the crowd had gathered outside the wardrobe shop.

"Make way!" Victor shouted. "What is going on to send you herding together like this? What is happening?"

By the time he'd asked the question, however, he and Margot had gotten through to the door and he stepped in. Suddenly he turned, pushing Margot back.

"No," he said, shock draining his voice to a whisper. "Go back, away from this."

But she'd already seen enough—the blood spattered over the walls and bolts of fabric, the many gashes and the torn flesh in the still body lying beneath an overturned sewing table. Margot would never be able to forget the sight of Pamela Laurie's body, or the horror of seeing the scissors protruding from the woman's throat.

Chapter Eleven

There was a trembling slowness about the way Margot moved that afternoon. She could feel herself walking around and even talking to people, but she wasn't physically aware of doing it. She saw herself being transported by her still-strong limbs and heard her voice respond to questions, but she just didn't have it in her to pay any more attention than that.

This seemed to be a common affliction among the cast, many of whom were weeping openly despite their previous expressions of disgust or annoyance at Pamela. It seemed that the woman had more than a few friends among the members of the company.

But Margot couldn't help but be struck by the cynical thought that they might be weeping for fear that any one of them could be next.

Sitting in the opera greenroom, the television on low in one corner, a few members of the ensemble waited mutely for their turn to talk to the policemen conducting the investigation. Margot sat on a low couch staring at the cup of cold coffee in her hand, grateful that she had the warmth of Bellamy's arm around her shoulder to keep her from falling apart.

Even though she knew it wasn't possible, the violence seemed to be following a pattern that included Tom Gleason. Anne had been attacked, her career nearly ruined, then the young carpenter had fallen to his death and now this, another incident in an accelerating pattern of violence. She felt as though she were the cause of it, the catalyst for this senseless destruction and despair. Yet that couldn't be so. She had nothing to do with it other than arriving just before it began.

On the television, "PM San Francisco" was presenting a demonstration of Halloween baking. The hosts were chuckling gleefully at the decorating tips. It was all so inane, so pointless to be prattling on about pumpkin cake while things like this were taking place in the city.

"I can't stand watching those people," she told Bellamy quietly. "It's so stupid to be watching television at a time like this."

"No, it's normal," he told her. He tightened his grip on her shoulder, drawing her slightly closer in an attempt to warm her chilled mood. "People seek refuge in the banal when disaster strikes. What could be more banal than a TV talk show?"

He sighed and rested his cheek against the top of her head for a moment, wishing he could take her shock and pain into his own body like a sponge soaking up water. He hadn't even met Pamela, and he'd already absorbed a death far more personal than this and lived. But he knew Margot's shock, and he felt pain in the empty, searching look in her eyes.

"I didn't know her," she said. "Not really, and we argued for most of the time that I did, but...well, I suppose it's like losing a relative who you never really liked. She was still family in a way."

"I know." Short answers were best in these situations, he knew. People who offered explanations or profound disclaimers ended up sounding pompous and condescending. All she needed was to know that he was there and that he wanted to help.

"*Do* you know?" she asked him. "Really?"

"I know what you mean," he replied. "But I don't feel what you feel. I can't know that because I didn't know her. So I won't say that I know what you're feeling."

"Yeah, I hate when people say they know how you feel."

"When my wife died," he began, then stopped to clear his throat. He continued more quietly. "When my wife died, one of her idiot friends said he knew how I felt. So I broke his nose."

"You what?" Margot's voice rose a bit, gaining a bit of color in response to his matter-of-fact statement.

"Decked him. I shouldn't have, but it sure felt good." He laughed quietly.

"You broke his nose," she marveled. "I wouldn't have thought you were the type."

"You would have hit him, too, if you knew him."

Margot felt a little better after that. She needed conversation to keep her from thinking of the blood and the gleaming handle of the shears.

"Turn him off!" somebody shouted, making an exaggerated gagging sound. "Don't torture us."

"Who?" Margot looked up and then at the television. Martin Andrews, an impersonator and Las Vegas headliner was on the show singing something in a borrowed voice which Margot didn't recognize. "Him? Victor was just talking about him. He was in the company, right?"

"Marty A-hole," Connie proclaimed, sitting on her other side. "He was in the company our first year."

"I wouldn't pick him as an opera singer."

"He thought he was, though." Connie laughed. "They let him go. Wouldn't you know it, he went on to become a millionaire by imitating celebrities."

"The one thing he didn't have to imitate was a jerk," David Trierweiller put in. "He was a natural at that."

"Even a bigger one than you, Trier," Neil Roberts, the stage manager, said.

Victor had begun saying something about Neil when we were interrupted, Margot thought then. The memory brought her to attention at Bellamy's side. What had Victor been about to tell her?

"Take a jump, Neil," the tenor snapped, though not without humor. "So, you're a writer," he said to Bellamy, "what do you think is going on here? Are we all being set up for butchery? Is that what he's doing?"

"If he is, a tenor would logically be next," Bellamy offered. "Of course, if I were writing it, he'd go after the director."

A small burst of laughter came in response, showing how far the healing process had already come. Margot found that any excuse to raise her spirits was welcome. Still, she kept her eye on the stage manager while she laughed.

But she still couldn't overcome the image of the blood, and her interview with Sergeant Terry didn't help her efforts to, either.

"I wanted to talk to both of you together because you live near each other," the sergeant said as he ushered them into the room he was using to talk to the cast.

"Yes, we do," Bellamy said as they sat across the table from him. "Why?"

"I want the two of you to stick together until we have this thing solved. You're alone out there, and I heard about the carpenter who died. We're going to take special care with his autopsy because I'm sure his death is part of the larger picture. Our boy has paid more attention to you, Miss Wylde, than to anyone else so far."

"But he can't be after me alone," she said.

"No, it seems that he's after the company. We'll check into the dead woman's life now and maybe we'll find something helpful. I don't know. There is a pattern, however."

The policeman looked seriously at Margot, drumming his fingers on the table between them.

"You were right about Taylor," he said after a moment. "This isn't for public consumption. We want to let the killer think that the L.A. police still have Jerome Taylor's death down as an accident."

"It wasn't?" Bellamy asked.

"No. In fact, the L.A. coroner's report from the autopsy shows that Taylor was struck in the throat before the supposed accident. There was massive damage to his larynx consistent with the blow of a blunt instrument. Might have been a club of some kind, or even a fist, but he was struck first and then pushed through the glass."

"So he was the first murder," Margot said.

"That's right," Sergeant Terry said. "The Los Angeles police have come up empty, so it looks like the whole thing moved up here when he died. We thought it was someone in the company. Now we're fairly positive. Do you remember if anyone in the company was missing when Jerome Taylor died?"

"Well, Daniel was out with a cold," Margot began. "And I think that Neil might have been gone that day, too. I didn't even consider it until just now, but I'm sure he was gone."

"Neil Roberts?" Terry interjected.

"Yes, I'm sure he was on vacation. Why, do you know him?"

"Oh, yes, we've had him in before. Him and his buddy, a guy named Andrews—he's a big shot now—they got hauled in on cocaine possession charges. We couldn't prove anything on Roberts, and the opera covered his ass for him, but the charges stuck on his pal."

"Martin Andrews?"

"Yes, is that name significant?"

"No, except that it keeps coming up. Victor mentioned his being let go from the company, but he didn't mention drug charges."

"I think we can rule him out," the policeman said. "The guy's worth several million. Neil Roberts is worth a look, however. You never know what a druggy might do."

"Do you think he might be the one?"

"Was anyone else gone then?"

"No, other than Daniel he was the only one that I can think of," Margot said. "But I would hate to have him jailed on my word."

"Don't worry, we'll check him out," the policeman assured her. "Once again, you've been a great help to us."

"Will you arrest him?" Bellamy asked.

"We'll put a tail on him and check out his alibi. There's not enough evidence for an arrest yet."

"That doesn't exactly make people around here safe, though, does it?"

"Like I told you, stick together. It's the same advice I'm giving everyone. Just don't go anywhere alone."

THE SEA POUNDED against the shore and a rumbling sound like thunder rolled across the land. From where Margot stood at the edge of the cliff, the whole world appeared to be made of water all moving toward her. She was at the edge of everything, a place where the difference between life and death was a matter of one wrong step, one misjudgment.

Her home was white and pristine inside, every wall covered seamlessly with enamel primer and glowing like a canvas awaiting the artist's brush. Some of her furniture—a couch, chair and two tables—had arrived already and sat wrapped in plastic in the center of the bare floor. Tomorrow the walls would have color, but the carpet installers would not arrive until Monday. Then she would have the opportunity to put in the rest of her furniture, hang pictures, unpack books and put her clothing away in the place she now called home.

She had far too many formal gowns for a woman her age. She'd decided that upon her return from the theater that evening. Three dozen of them, unless her count was off, and she wasn't even fond of formal events. Too many dresses and not enough blue jeans. That was her life up until now.

But she wanted more than that. Where once she had yearned for international acclaim and the chance to sing the big roles in opera, she now wanted a hearth and a cup of hot chocolate and a book. She wanted the wind whistling past the eaves while she sat cozy in her own home. She wanted more blue jeans and fewer formal gowns.

International acclaim was much easier to obtain than any of that. And easier still than obtaining the companionship of an enigmatic man like Edward Bellamy.

Walking along the cliff toward Bellamy's house in the warm glow of the evening sun, Margot wondered what she'd have to do to bribe Bellamy into playing piano at her housewarming party. She would have to think of something.

He was waiting for her on his flagstone patio before the broad windows of his house. The wind blew his open coat back like wings and tossed his hair wildly. He looked so strong as she approached him, like granite against the wind, yet at one time he'd been weak enough to strike a man for an innocuous comment. There were so many complications in him that she wasn't sure she'd ever know the man at all.

"Everything intact?" he asked as she joined him.

"Yes, the place is so clean and white that it's kind of scary." She slipped her arm around his waist, daring to make contact for fear that it might never be made if she didn't. "It seemed like they'd never be done, and now they're suddenly at the end of everything."

"Well, it's always darkest before the dawn." He put his arm around her shoulder, holding her to him.

"And a half-empty bottle is also half-full," she countered.

"And a fool and his money are soon parted."

"What?"

"It's true, isn't it?"

"Yes, but, well... Look before you leap. How's that?"

"And yet he who hesitates is lost."

"Yes, he is," she said. She turned her face up to him, examining the lines in his face and wondering what he saw in hers.

"Don't you have another one?" His smile was warm and gentle.

"No," she said. "That one's good enough."

"Yes, it is." He brought two fingers to her chin, touching her lightly as he lowered his lips to hers and kissed her with the tenderness of a warm summer breeze just brushing her skin.

They stood for a moment, their lips inches apart, eyes gazing hungrily, and then they parted, aware that a barrier had been breached but not wanting things to move too fast.

"I made a light supper," he said. "I didn't expect you to be very hungry."

"Oh, I don't know, Pamela said I should—" She cut herself off, fighting a brief sense of desperation. "She said I had lost weight," she finished. "That I should eat more so I would fit the costumes."

"I've got some Ben & Jerry's for dessert."

"Okay. I think that will do."

They walked into the house still linked together, parting only long enough to get through the door and then moving instinctively together like teenagers who had just learned the pleasure of touching and being touched.

They ate in the kitchen, at the large mission table before the window. During their supper, the sun went down and revealed a host of stars twinkling over the calm sea, which was already beginning to form a mist on its surface. The mist crept along the rippling face of the ocean and rose with careful slowness up the face of the precipice until it reached the top and moved over the flagstones to the wall of Edward Bellamy's house.

Only ankle deep, the fog provided a dreamy landscape for the remainder of their meal, stealing the world away from view and isolating them within its icy shroud.

"Why did you get out of music?"

Relaxed in the large, comfortable room, Margot asked Bellamy the question most on her mind since speaking to Victor Grimaldi. She couldn't conceive of anyone wanting to leave music, not voluntarily, and wondered why he had.

"Why did you get into it?" he replied. She wasn't sure from the serious expression on his face whether he was avoiding her question or answering it.

"Me? Well, I enjoy singing," she said. "I just always have."

"And you have the talent for it. That helps."

"Sure, but talent without desire won't get you anywhere."

"Which is why I left music. I'd rather talk about you, Margot."

"But Victor said that you were very talented."

"Victor's memory isn't what it used to be." Bellamy smiled, turning slightly to look at her and folding his arms over his chest. "I was a composition major, and I felt I could do better with words than music."

"I find it inconceivable that anyone would give up music." She tilted her head slightly and regarded him closely, waiting either for a response that would answer her questions or another turn in the conversation.

"I haven't given it up. I play."

"Victor says that you write your books as though they were music."

"All that requires is a sense of rhythm." He laughed. "Besides, you can write a book all alone, but composing music requires dealing with an orchestra at some time or another."

"And you work alone."

"I work best alone," he said rising and going to a window. "That's why I don't write plays or scripts. I hate having to explain what I've written to people."

"I guess that does make sense," she told him. "And, if it means anything, I do think you made a good career move. You certainly write well."

"Thank you. It means quite a bit to hear you say that. In fact, it may be the highest praise I've ever gotten." He spoke with a boyish sincerity coloring his voice, and was unable to restrain the pleased smile that came to his lips.

"Of course, I haven't finished the book, but you certainly have me hooked. Victor says that *Whiteout* is an opera—musically speaking, that is."

"An opera." He scowled slightly, letting his lips form an impertinent half smile. "Well, considering the source, I suppose that's a compliment. I would probably have to agree, though. It is awfully melodramatic."

"There you go with melodrama again!" she exclaimed. "Is melodrama so wrong?"

"Not in an opera. In literature, unless accompanied by humor, it is generally regarded as something less than good."

"What about this little melodrama we're involved in now? How do you think it'll end?"

"I don't know. I just wish there was some way to narrow the field a bit more. Other than ruling out Anne Lewis and Tom Gleason, we're still at sea."

"Which leaves Daniel, though I doubt he'd go this far to sell tickets, and Neil Roberts, who may or may not be so lost in cocaine paranoia that he decides to kill off the whole company. Or, of course, there are any number of ex-employees who might bear the company a grudge."

"But not a grudge against you?"

"No, I don't know any of them," she admitted. "And he's gone to a lot of trouble to get at me, hasn't he?"

"A whole lot of trouble. I can't see why, either. The opera could be stopped without killing anyone, so the person must have a grudge against the people there specifically. But he has no reason to have paid so much attention to you alone."

"Are you suggesting that he may be paying separate attention to me for some reason other than the opera?"

"Maybe," he said, as the telephone on his desk rang. "Can you think of any reason someone might be after you?"

He left the couch to answer the phone, his question hanging in the air as he picked up the receiver. Then he frowned and turned away, saying something else as he tapped his fist rapidly on the desk top. He hung up the phone and stood hunched over it for a moment as though a great weight had dropped onto his shoulders.

"What is it?" Margot began to rise. "What happened?"

He didn't say anything, but, in a sudden burst of rage, he picked up the telephone and slammed it onto his desk with an anguished shout. Then he lifted the damaged instrument and threw it, the cord popping from the wall to trail behind like the tail of a kite. The telephone slammed into the bookcase and clattered to the floor.

Bellamy turned then, his face totally calm, almost bereft of expression. He looked as though he had forgotten something and wasn't sure what it was, wasn't even sure where he was.

"Damn," he said, blankly. "I broke my phone."

"What happened?" Margot rushed to his side, grasping his arm and staring up into his vacant eyes.

"That was Pressman," he said. His eyes began to shimmer, tears welling within them to be furiously blinked away. "He said that—that, Victor was attacked tonight."

"Victor! My God, is he dead?"

"No, not quite. He's in surgery now. That bastard cut Victor's throat!"

He fought to find something else to say, but there was nothing. The man who made his living with words could do nothing more to express himself than take Margot in his arms and hold her as though the world were ending.

Chapter Twelve

Bellamy drove rapidly along the coastal roadway to the city. He could only thank God that Margot had agreed to stay behind and wait. He didn't want company, not now. He was far too angry.

Bellamy was not a man of great temper. He didn't hold in his displeasures as some did but expressed them immediately, and he did not let anything that displeased him grate on his nerves. But the news that Victor had been attacked that evening in the opera house had struck Bellamy nearly as hard as the news of Kay's death on the very road over which he was racing to the city. He had been unable to deal with it in any way other than a strictly physical one. So, just as he'd struck a well-intentioned— though unlikable—man at the funeral, he'd destroyed his telephone.

Unfortunately, he'd done it in front of Margot, and he hated the possibility that she might think ill of him because of that outburst.

Still, even now, the thought of a man in his sixties having to fend off a maniac with a knife made Bellamy so mad that he could easily have torn the steering wheel out of the car. Rather than do that, he gripped the wheel with knuckle-whitening force and pushed the accelerator to the floor, rocketing his vehicle along the twisted road through the thickening fog.

MARGOT FELT at a loss in Bellamy's large house. He'd told her that he would call as soon as he knew something about the musician's condition and that she should make herself at home while he was gone. Still, she felt like an intruder here without him. Kay's clothing was still hanging in the bedroom, after all, just as his memories of her clearly hung over his mind.

She took their ice-cream bowls back to the kitchen, then took a soda from the fridge and stood with it for a long time, looking out the window in the direction of the sea. There was nothing but fog to be seen through the window. The fog made everything lonely, darkening her mood into one of gloomy introspection.

The more she looked, the more ominous the fog became, capable of hiding a great variety of dangers within its icy mist. There might be someone out there right now, in fact.

Margot drew the draperies quickly, but still the feeling of eyes upon her persisted. The killer could be anyone, and he could be out there now.

She'd come a long way to get to this point in her life, but her success didn't seem worth it with the gray mist moving slowly outside and a feeling of dread in her heart. Her move back home to the United States had turned into a macabre excursion into fear with only Bellamy's presence to give it some light. Everything she did seemed tainted by the death surrounding her, and less desirable because of it.

Everything but Edward Bellamy.

But he was an enigma. Outwardly cheerful, with a guarded friendliness bespeaking a solitary life, he possessed a dark soul that seemed immune to any efforts to open a window on its shuttered existence. It was clear that his dead wife's memory haunted him. He must have loved her terribly to be so greatly affected after three years. Margot didn't expect him to forget his feelings for the woman, but she would have thought that the man could at least talk about her after this much time.

But then Victor had said that Kay had left him before her death. Perhaps that was the key to Bellamy's obsession. But why had she left him? And why was Victor so convinced that Kay had not been the right woman for Bellamy? It was clear that Bellamy still thought she had been.

His solitary life wasn't a choice but a sentence that he'd imposed on himself. His feelings were something that he assigned to the characters in his books, hoping to be rid of them.

But he wasn't rid of them. When he'd thrown his telephone across the room, Margot had been shocked. He was too rational a man to give in to such base impulses. But she realized that it was just such a man, rational and self-contained, who would be lacking any other outlet when confronted with such a shock as the one he'd had tonight. Clearly, Victor Grimaldi was more than a friend to Bellamy, but Margot wondered if he'd ever admitted as much to himself. He was probably every bit as surprised by his sudden outburst as she had been.

How could she get through to the emotions he tried so hard to contain? If their earlier kiss was any indication, he did want her to get through. But where would they find the trust necessary to create such a connection?

Margot was probably as ill equipped to deal with emotions as he was, and she faced this fact ruefully now. Her life had been easily led and men followed her everywhere she went. As a performer, she had made peace with her physical appearance long ago. Margot knew that some might consider her beautiful, and so was prepared for the advances her looks engendered. But she had become immune to them over time, never certain how honest the attention was or how permanent people meant it to be.

She had gotten to the point where she was no longer looking for love or expecting it to come looking for her. Love had become something she sang about on stage just as Bellamy put his emotions on paper. Only by seeing that disability in Bellamy's life did she realize that she was similarly afflicted.

Now she wanted love more than anything. She wanted Edward Bellamy's love. But it seemed that he'd already given it to an unreachable woman named Kay.

Thinking of Edward Bellamy helped to drive her fear back, though it could not dispel it entirely. No, she couldn't escape her fear until the killer was safely behind bars, but she determined to calm her nerves a bit by gaining a bit of elevation. If she was upstairs, at least the maniac stalking the opera couldn't break directly in upon her. He would have a harder time watching her up there, too.

The climb up the curved staircase past the wall of glass was unnerving, however, and she made the trip quickly with her heart thudding in her chest. In this fog, anyone close enough to see her would also be close enough for her to see him, after all. Still, she arrived at the second floor feeling breathless with relief for having made it to safety once more.

She went to the guest room, its bedding still rumpled by last night's activity, and changed into her nightgown and robe. Then she took Connie's copy of *Whiteout* and sat, intending to finish the novel while she waited for Bellamy.

There was no telephone in the spare bedroom, though, so she opened the door to his. If she left his door and hers ajar, she would hear his call.

But the moonlight that flooded down above the fog lit the bedroom with an etched clarity, and she could see his closet standing open with a chair pulled up before it heaped with clothing.

Feeling like a spy, but remembering his invitation to make herself at home, she switched on the bedroom light and walked in.

The closet that had held Kay's clothing was bare now. He had removed everything, hangers and all, and had thrown the clothes over the back of the chair. A cardboard box on the floor contained two pairs of shoes and some other items.

This proved that there was hope. After three years without moving them, he had finally been prompted to make an attempt at exorcising his dead wife's ghost. Just as with the telephone, physical action had been his method of emotional release.

Margot felt an unusual thrill within her, a warmth that grew with her conviction that it was she who had prompted his action. He wanted to make room for her in his heart as he might make room in a closet. He truly wanted to let her in.

Margot put her book down on his bed and walked around the room, shamelessly examining it as she hadn't done the night before. She didn't think that he spent much time here, for it still bore the look of a woman's room in its pastel shades and French provincial furniture.

The piano, a full-size grand, filled the area before the window, clearly the centerpiece of the room. What reason they might have had to place it here and not in a public area of the house wasn't anything Margot wanted to speculate on. She could imagine, however, and she smiled at her imagination's work.

When she walked around the piano, she saw a book lying on the bench and picked it up idly. It was his wedding album. Since she was already an intruder, she couldn't find any reason not to compound the crime, and so she opened the album.

Kay Bellamy had been a stunning woman. A ravishing honey blonde, she dominated every one of the rather standard pictures in the book. She was nearly a foot shorter than Bellamy and possessed looks that would have given her an instant career in movies or television, and could have obtained her the adoration of any man. On a physical level it was obvious why she dominated his thoughts. And there was a light in her eyes, evident even in the photographs, that bespoke intelligence and determination. She knew what she wanted and would surely get it.

Margot felt a bit daunted by the task of overcoming the woman in the wedding photographs. She paged through the book, noting that Victor Grimaldi had acted as best man for the wedding, and easily picking out the tall, still-shapely woman with silver hair and chiseled features as Bellamy's mother. His father had apparently died before the wedding, for his mother was never pictured with anyone. Kay's parents were average-looking people, showing no sign of their capacity to produce a daughter as beautiful as she had been.

When she reached the end of the book, a stack of loose newspaper clippings and stationery slid out, nearly falling to the floor before she stopped them. Feeling like a treasure hunter who'd reached the X in her map, Margot carried the book and papers over to the bed and began reading.

Margot was shocked to learn that Kay Bellamy had died in a car accident on the road leading from the house to the city. The news stories indicated excessive speed as the cause—she'd gone too wide on an inward turn and crashed to the rocks below. She was identified as the "estranged wife" of author Edward Bellamy, but not the "ex-wife."

She died two months before the publication of his novel, *Whiteout,* a book clearly meant for her to read.

Amid the clippings Margot found a postcard sent from San Francisco two days before the accident.

I'll be there for the rest of my things on Thursday. Have the papers signed for me then.

Kay

Perhaps this was at the core of the situation. She had come for her clothing on the day she was killed. She had come expecting something—presumably the divorce papers—to be signed, but they weren't. Edward Bellamy hadn't wanted to let her go and had clung to his last desperate hope of maintaining the marriage by not signing the divorce papers.

And she died on her way back to the city after that meeting.

Margot found her mind lost in reflection on the mysterious tug-of-war that love can become. Had he loved her so madly that he couldn't understand the fact that he couldn't keep her? Had he lost his artist's insight on the human condition when it came to real life and tried to bind her love to him with legal documentation?

And having failed, was he now unwilling to offer his love to anyone for fear that he would again become so possessive that he might be blind to his loved one's needs?

Maybe Bellamy hated opera because his life so closely resembled one.

Margot put the album back on the bench, pausing to play a few notes on the keys before her. The music had a melancholy sound in the still air; single notes of music reached out and died alone in the misty night.

Margot turned to leave the room just as the telephone rang on the bedside table. She rushed over to pick up the receiver and sat on the edge of the bed.

"He made it through surgery," Bellamy told her, his voice conveying an immense sense of relief and fatigue. "The doctor said it would have been worse if the killer had used a sharper blade. He said it appeared to be a wound from a dull hatchet or sword of some kind, more of a chop than a cutting wound."

"The sword is missing at the theater," Margot told him, her own heart suddenly beating rapidly with a released energy. "It was a prop sword, real but not very sharp."

"That's probably it then. They arrested your stage manager on suspicion. Haven't charged him yet," he said.

"Do they have any proof against Neil?" She didn't know the quiet manager well, but he certainly didn't seem the type to commit murder.

"Opportunity, mainly. And he failed a drug test after they arrested him."

"Yes, he surely had the opportunity," she mused. "And you know, I've been thinking about something. Everyone who was attacked was injured in the throat. Do you think there was jealousy involved? I mean, if Roberts was a failed singer, he might have gone over the edge and tried to get rid of those who succeeded at it."

"That's a damn nice theory," Bellamy responded. "I'll pass it along to the cops."

"Is Victor going to make it? Did you talk to the doctor?"

"Yes, it looks good. His vocal chords were cut a bit, so he'll have trouble talking, but he should pull through if he's motivated."

"He's got an opera to premiere," Margot exclaimed. "Of course he's motivated!"

"God, I'd never have thought an opera could save someone's life," he replied happily. "I'll be back in half an hour or so."

"Good. I'll wait up," she said, lying back against his pillow. His house seemed lonely without him in it, and she longed for his return.

"I'll hurry," he promised.

"No, don't hurry," Margot said quickly. The thought of that road and the fog and his penchant for driving too fast brought a sudden and horrible picture to her mind. "You sound tired. Drive carefully."

"I'm beat," he admitted. "You know, we don't have very good luck with dinner engagements, do we?"

"We'll have more opportunities," she told him. "If you'd like."

"I would. Don't wait up if you're tired."

"No, I'll wait. I've got a good book to keep me company."

She hung up the phone and stretched out on his king-size bed. Everything seemed brighter now, the fog outside a pleasant mist rather than the enshrouding gloom it had appeared earlier. And she was tired, too. The strain of not knowing what was happening with Victor and its release left her feeling numb with fatigue.

She began to read, but lay back instead and looked up at the ceiling. This was his bed—*their* bed—but she didn't feel out of place in it. She felt she'd come home in a way, as if her presence here was fated from the start. The warm sense of belonging deepened into a deliciously sexual feeling of being here in his house, his bed. Though waking naked in his guest room had been sensually pleasant, this feeling of lounging on his bed was charged with a deeper arousal that made her long for the time when she might tell him what she felt and hear his words echo her desire.

She drifted, her eyes slipping shut to the sound of music, an aria sung to the mists that softened the air outside the bedroom window. She didn't worry about the trick her imagination might be playing with song, for it could only be her imagination. There was no one to threaten her within these walls, no more shadowy assailants waiting to cut the song from her throat. There was only this soft bed and the soft sound of the music in the mist and the feeling of love that grew in her heart.

She dreamed of him standing before her. There was an impression of nakedness but the dream remained tantalizingly unclear, misty, leaving the two of them standing and looking into each other's eyes. But then he turned, staring toward another form. A woman sang behind him, her song so plaintively sad and so beautiful that even Margot looked.

It was Kay, reaching for him, singing her love while Margot's own voice was suddenly frozen in her throat. She was unable to make her desires known, unable to ask him to stay with her and not chase after the ghost who sang in the mist at his back. Bellamy walked away, fading as he did, leaving her alone again.

Margot awoke to darkness with a strange pressure on her chest. The covers had been pulled over her, and for a moment she thought she'd returned to the guest bedroom and put herself to bed. But the sound of breathing came to her then, and she became aware that she was still in his bed, and she was not alone.

Bellamy was lying at her side, his head resting on her breast as he slept grasping her hand in his. He had found her in his bed and covered her. Then he had lain at her side fully clothed and atop the covers, resting beside her as though it was the most natural thing in the world for him to do.

She stroked his hair in the darkness, feeling more alive than ever before in the glow of the trust he'd placed in her. She'd been right, of course, for his actions had again taken the place of his words and he'd expressed himself more eloquently in sleep than his waking mind could ever allow him to do.

Margot turned her face down to kiss the top of his head lightly, knowing that the dream had been nothing more than illusion. His ghosts had no more hold here.

MARGOT AWOKE ALONE in the large bed. Refreshed, but somewhat stiff from sleeping on her back with his head lying protectively over her, she threw back the blanket he'd covered her with on top of the comforter and got out of bed. The sky, gloriously clear and brimming with sunlight, lay open before her as she walked around the bed, as if the large window between her and the magnificent vista outside had completely evaporated.

She was aware that the shower had been running only after it stopped. A moment later, the door of the master bath opened and Bellamy stepped through wearing his robe and rubbing his hair dry with a large, thick towel.

"Water's still hot," he told her. A smile flickered at the corner of his expressive mouth, but stopped. "I, uh, I hope you don't mind," he said haltingly, then added with a shrug that seemed designed to push away any tenderness that had been trying to come out, "Well, it's my bed, after all."

"I don't mind." Margot stepped toward him, well aware that neither her nightgown nor robe were designed for modesty in such bright light as the sun was providing. "You should have woken me up."

"No, I couldn't disturb you." He stepped back a bit and then smiled broadly. "That book would put anyone to sleep."

"It's a wonderful book." Margot moved toward him, placing her hand on his upper arm and staring up into his eyes. "But sad."

"I'll write a comedy next," he assured her.

"No, don't make jokes," she said, grasping his arm firmly. The glorious sun and the wonderful feeling of warmth and desire he gave her made her bold. "It's a beautiful, expressive book written by a beautiful but haunted man."

"I don't know what you mean," he said, losing his composure again.

"Yes, you do. You didn't do it, you know," she said. Margot reached out to stroke the side of his face lightly, her fingers stopping at the corner of his mouth. "It wasn't your fault that she died."

"Of course not," he snapped. Bellamy pulled away, taking two steps toward the door before she stopped him with a hand on his forearm.

"You loved her, that's all. There's no crime in that. You just didn't realize that you couldn't hold on to her."

"I know, Margot. Let's not talk about that," he blurted out. His lips compressed into a white line while his eyes became blue ice. "It's done with."

"No, it's not!" Holding him by both arms now, she pulled against his resistance. "And it won't be over until you talk about it. Please, Bellamy, I don't know everything, but I can tell what you've been putting yourself through since she died. You wrote that book to get her back, to say that you were sorry, and she didn't even have the chance to read it. You should have told her what you felt instead of waiting for her to read it. You should have said it out loud."

"I did!" he exclaimed, his face twisting in torment. "Every day, every hour, but it didn't help. I just couldn't get through to her. I couldn't prove myself to her! Margot, I tried."

"Maybe she didn't want to let you in. Maybe it was her all along, not you. How could you know?"

"You don't know me," he said angrily. "I write for hours, never coming out, leaving people to their own devices, and they get lonely, damn lonely, waiting for me to pay attention to them. I didn't even know that I wasn't paying attention until she told me! I was so stupid that I didn't even know."

"But even Victor said that you and Kay were mismatched. He thought the divorce was inevitable, Bellamy, and he's a very perceptive man! You and Kay were too dissimilar! Right from the start, you were just too far apart to ever reach each other. Can't you see that?"

"I should have changed."

"Nobody can change his basic character. Nobody. We are what we are and we learn to live with it. That's what life's about, and if two people aren't right for each other, no amount of twisting around will change it."

"It's hard," he said in obvious misery.

"I know," she said. "It's hard to give up on your love. I know because I know that I couldn't give you up any more than I can give up singing. I don't know why or how, but I love you! But I can't be in love with a man haunted by past mistakes. If you're too scared to try love again, at least you can admit that you feel it.''

"I do feel it," he said. "I love you, Margot."

"Then don't worry about doing it right or wrong, because there is no right or wrong way to love," she said, circling him with her arms. "I want what happened the other night to happen over and over again for the rest of our lives. I want to go to bed with you and wake up with you every day. I even want to be lonely while you're writing just so that I can be glad when you've finished your work. I want to be with you forever."

"Oh, Margot, I love you so much," he whispered, staring into her eyes. "I'd stop breathing if you were harmed in any way by anything that I ever did. And especially by what I didn't do. God, Margot, I've thought about you every waking hour since we met and spent most nights dreaming about you."

"It's not so hard to admit," she said, slipping her arms around his back and resting her cheek against his chest.

"Last night was the first complete night's sleep I've had in three years," he told her. "Just being that close was medicine."

"You don't know how much I wanted to hear that," she whispered against the silken fabric of his robe. "You know, you're not getting an easy deal by hooking up with me, either. I have my career, too."

"Maybe we're made for each other," he said. "Maybe we've both got enough going that we won't come to resent the time each of us has to spend alone. You're not Kay, after all. And I don't want you to be her." He tipped her head back with one hand and twined the fingers of the other through her long brown tresses. "I just want to be sure I don't make any mistakes. Because I know now that I can't go back and fix them later."

"Just pretend that I'm a blank sheet of paper," Margot said, meeting his smoldering gaze with one of her own. "Write on me, Bellamy, and I'll tell you if it needs revision."

He dipped his head to kiss her then, a damp lock of his hair cooling her cheek as their arms circled and their bodies were pressed together. Her hands found the belt of his robe and tugged it free even while he was slipping the fabric of her sheer robe over her nightgown, baring her shoulders to his kisses as her lips found his chest.

They moved in tandem to the bed, never losing touch of each other as they both fell under the spell of the rapturous delight they found in the nearness, the warmth, of their bodies. The sight of Bellamy's well-muscled body inflamed her as he moved to untie the ribbon at her throat, creating a spark that exploded at the touch of his hands on the expectant surface of her skin and the warmth of his lips on her breasts.

The room disappeared around them, leaving them in the glow of sunlight like a liquid fire in the air, their bodies and minds united until at last they found release from all uncertainty and lay spent in each other's arms.

"I love you," he whispered. "I love you. Love you."

"I wouldn't revise that one bit," she said.

"It is easy to say with a little practice." He chuckled softly, kissing her forehead tenderly. "I think I'll say it more often."

And though they might have said it again and again all morning, there was little time for anything besides a quick shower together and a pleasant drive into town, where they found themselves in the center of the dervish of activity that consumed the opera house.

"I CANNOT COMPETENTLY jump into the fray so late in the game without your assistance. Absolutely not." The concert master, Thomas Brent, met them nearly on the threshold of the theater to accost Bellamy with questions about the new score. The man wore a harried expression quite out of place given his refined features. His forehead wrinkled into furrows of concern that rode high into the bald dome of his head.

"Please, Bellamy, come along. The orchestra is waiting to begin rehearsal with no notes on the new phrasing."

"Okay, I'm right behind you," the author said to the worried violinist. Then, turning to Margot, he said, "I won't be long."

"I can't rehearse until they've sorted themselves out, anyway," she replied. "Have fun."

He screwed his face into an amused scowl and walked into the theater with a small wave.

The company was in a touchy mood all around. While the costume crew had reacted to Pamela's death with a certain inertia, the orchestra had become restive and prickly after their leader's injuries. They were jumpy and quarrelsome, objecting to each change of phrasing the new lyrics demanded, more from a simple need to object than from any concrete musical problem.

Bellamy found the experience of dealing with an orchestra every bit as aggravating as he'd expected, and he was at last fully relieved of any latent doubts about his move out of music as a profession. Their picky objections, and their need to direct those objections at him regardless of the fact that he hadn't written the score, only the lyrics, made him feel as anxious as they were. No, he would not have had a long career in music even if he had the talent for it.

Once the orchestra had its questions answered, Bellamy was horrified to find that he was expected to be there for the rehearsals with each and every singer as well. If it weren't for his friendship with Victor, he'd tell them to take a hike. But he couldn't duck the obligation, and so he refilled his cup of coffee and sat in the front row of the theater and watched as the first group of the chorus gathered to sing through their numbers.

He could only hope that Margot was having a better day than he was.

"No, dear, to your left. Stage right." Daniel Pressman consulted his script once more and then peered at Margot over his half glasses. "You can't cross left or you'll be upstaged when they enter at the end of your song."

Margot moved to her new position on the rehearsal stage, which had been marked with masking tape to show the placement of the set pieces on the main stage. The rehearsal space was not a stage at all, but one half of the dance studio. It could only approximate the area they would be using on the real stage.

"Please, people, I'd like to have this blocking down before midnight so that we can have our weekend." Pressman spoke in the edgy manner of someone who truly needed a weekend off. "It's bad enough that we have no stage manager now, but we've got to stumble through without a proper musical director as well. Let us all work together and get through with it."

"I can't believe Neil tried to slash the maestro," David Trierweiller said. He was standing to the rear of the space, in a position that was marked "offstage" by a line of tape on the floor. "What's he got to gain from any of this?"

"What does it matter as long as he's in custody?" Pressman said. "Now, may we continue?"

"Why didn't you fire him when you fired Martin Andrews?" Margot asked. "I understand that they were both dealing drugs."

"No, dear, not at all," Pressman said. "Please, continue with your reading."

"Wait, I heard that Neil and Martin were using cocaine," she insisted. "That's why Martin was released."

"Oh, sure." Pressman sighed. "They both were known to snort a line or two, but it had nothing to do with releasing Martin Andrews."

"So why did you release him?"

"He was a disruptive member of our little family, I'm afraid," Pressman said with distaste. "A singer of low talent, yet he insisted that he should be in the lead of all productions. He had a greater impression of his talents than anyone else, you see."

"And so you canned him?"

"He was a pain in the neck, and he assaulted and insulted every woman in the company at one time or another. The only woman who could stand him was poor Pamela, and even she overcame whatever delusion first convinced her that he was a person worth having anything to do with. Besides, as his current career shows, his talent was one of mimicry, not originality. He had no soul, no feeling of his own for the music." Pressman laughed, his script forgotten in his reminiscence. "Victor said that Martin would make a perfect lead if we could afford to hire another singer to sing the part for him first. That way he could mimic the singer's phrasing and thus put on a believable show. I think you can sense a certain lack of economic feasibility in that notion, can't you?"

"One for the price of two," Trierweiller said tiredly. "Can we get going?"

"Who fired him?" Margot asked.

"Victor, of course," Pressman said. "He is the musical director. I had no reason to release him aside from his
lack of acting ability. If we fired people because they can't
act, we would soon be devoid of people to put on the
operas. So, take your aria from the last two lines and cross
to the right so that David can come in with his reply. And
remember, our set will be done primarily with lighting, so
the sight lines are crucial. Okay, begin again."

And so they progressed, step by step, each of them trying hard to concentrate on their work while never quite
overcoming the urge to look over their shoulders. No
matter that a suspect was in jail, the seeds of fear had been
too well sown to be rooted out so easily.

At least now they were in sight of their goal. It was Friday, September twenty-ninth. The opera opened in two
weeks on Friday, October the thirteenth; soon they would
all be so busy that they would forget their fear in the excitement of the coming production.

Edward Bellamy's week with the opera had been a
mixed blessing. He counted becoming involved with
Margot Wylde as its sole high point. Today would have
been horrible if he hadn't known that Margot would soon
be on the stage in front of him, and he could sit back and
enjoy her beautiful voice once again.

Of course he had to listen to the chorus mumble
through his lyrics while the orchestra butchered Victor's
score before he could be granted the nirvana of Margot's
voice. He only hoped he could hold out that long before
he ran screaming from the theater.

He hadn't been joking when he told Margot that he
hated opera, although that wasn't entirely true. All the
years of watching his father work with the opera, the
times as a child being shuffled around backstage and
barely tolerated by the performers had given him a dark

view of the whole thing. But then his experience had been
with foreign-language operas, not those sung in English.
He was finding that, when he could understand the words,
he didn't really mind it so much. In fact, he could come
to like it.

Still, the singers before him weren't at ease with the
lyrics yet, and so they stumbled and mumbled and drove
him insane until finally, like a ray of sunshine erupting
into a dank crypt, Margot walked onto the stage.

"Thank God you're here," he called out.

"I hope you'll hold out," she replied, laughing. "I
don't have the words down yet."

"That's just fine," he said. "The band doesn't have the
notes down yet, either."

A small mumble of displeasure passed through the orchestra at that comment, giving him a fair bit of pleasure
after the harassment they'd given him earlier.

"Shall we begin?" the concert master said, standing
poised behind his podium.

"Whenever you're ready," Margot told him.

Margot's voice rang clear and strong in the empty hall,
a voice so filled with emotion that it seemed as though the
walls would crack under its glorious power.

In fact, it seemed as though she *was* having a physical
effect on the structure for a moment. Bellamy noticed that
the light beamed on the stage was wavering, moving as
though the steel lighting rail over the stage was being
shaken. Bellamy got up and walked around the orchestra
to the temporary steps leading up to the stage while Margot and the orchestra continued with the aria.

He couldn't see into the fly space above the stage
against the glare of the lights, but something told him that
it was important to investigate the small movements oc-

curring up there, so he mounted the stage and began walking back where he might see better.

Then, buried amid the sound of the music, Bellamy could hear a distinct snapping sound. The light on the stage shifted radically.

Bellamy sprinted toward Margot, not even sparing enough breath to shout a warning. He tackled her and rolled to the very edge of the stage before a steel pole filled with lighting instruments crashed to the boards where Margot had been standing. Glass from the shattered Fresnel lenses of the lights flew through the air like shrapnel, several pieces striking Bellamy's back.

Margot had been caught totally by surprise, but the sound of a thousand pounds of lighting equipment smashing to the stage quickly alerted her to what had happened. She lay beneath the shelter of Bellamy's body, knowing with horrified certainty that the deadly events at the opera house weren't yet completed.

Chapter Thirteen

Chaos erupted as Bellamy helped Margot rise to her feet. The cast members who had been nearby hurried in to investigate the noise and surrounded them with questions before either had a chance to catch their breaths.

The tumult finally brought Daniel Pressman, who surveyed the destroyed equipment and the splintered stage with dismay.

"What on earth is going on!" he shouted. "What is it that God has against this opera? Why us?"

"I don't think it was an act of God," Bellamy said as he walked over to one end of the lighting pole. "Why did both ends give way? I can see the chains on one end breaking, but not both at the same time. It came straight down."

He knelt to examine the broken end of the chain that had held up one end of the rack of lights. "Yes," he said, "I may be wrong, but this sure looks like it was cut most of the way through."

"Same here!" shouted one of the chorus members, holding up the chain on the far end in his hand.

"Somebody call that cop!" Pressman commanded. "Get him over here."

"I think we should get Margot out of here," Bellamy suggested. "He was aiming this thing at her, you know. He could have killed twenty people ten minutes earlier."

"You're saying that he was up there the whole time?" Pressman moved nervously away from the fallen lights, warily eyeing the dark spaces above the stage. "He could be up there now."

"No, because he knows we'll check out the flies as quickly as possible. He's long gone now," Bellamy assured the man. "But he had to be up there when it fell."

"Why?"

"Because he didn't cut all the way through the chains. They might have held for months before they broke if he hadn't forced them to give. He probably hung on to the catwalk and jumped on the bar until it snapped free.

"So he wanted to kill our lead?"

"Exactly."

"What?" Margot joined the two men, instinctively, grasping Bellamy's arm as she did. "Why does he want to kill me?"

"I don't know," Bellamy admitted. "But we do know that this time was deliberate. Maybe he attacked Anne because he mistook her for you."

"And the same with Pamela and Victor?"

"I don't know. But we should play it safe until we do," he told her. "I think you should get out of here and lock yourself up in my place for the weekend while the police work on things."

"And what about next week? Do you really think they'll have it wrapped up?"

"We'll cross that bridge when we get to it."

"It makes sense, dear," Pressman agreed. "We won't continue today anyway. The police will surely waste the rest of our day for us and I don't imagine anyone is in the mood to rehearse anymore at any rate. After Sergeant What's-his-name is finished with you, you guys just go ahead and leave. At least I'll have my stage manager back now. He couldn't very well have done this from jail."

Margot had to admit that she didn't feel very much like singing at the moment, and she did feel vulnerable on the open stage. She wouldn't be secure until she had four walls around her—four walls and a lock on the door.

"This was the first attack that didn't fit the pattern," she told Bellamy as they waited for the sergeant to question them.

"What do you mean?"

"Anne, Victor and Pamela were all attacked in the throat," she reminded him. "Their voices. This time he just wanted to smash me flat."

"He probably didn't expect that he would have a chance to get you alone."

"No, not now, that's for sure," she said. Margot leaned her head against Bellamy's shoulder, his nearness comforting her. "I wonder about Tom Gleason, too."

"Why?" Bellamy said. "He stumbled in the dark. And his wasn't a throat injury."

"No. And, just because this attack was directed at me, that doesn't mean that it's anything personal. He may be after all of the lead people at the opera."

"In which case, David Trierweiller has moved up to the top of the hit list."

"We'd better warn him."

"We'd better," Bellamy echoed.

"I HAVE A CONFESSION to make," Bellamy said.

They had just finished moving a couch, still wrapped in plastic, to its position beneath the window overlooking the sea in Margot's home. The carpeting had been laid in the living room and Margot's bedroom, leaving only two rooms uncarpeted of those whose floors were destined to be covered. Half of her furniture had been delivered as well, and was left standing in the middle of the room with a shipping bill left on top of the couch signed by one of the carpet installers.

"A confession? What's that?" Margot poked her fingernail through the plastic wrap on her couch and began peeling it away.

"I'm starting to like opera," he said. "You're winning me over."

"I am, or opera is?"

"You, mostly," he admitted. He helped tear the plastic free, wadding it up in a crinkly ball, which he carried over and stuffed into a paper grocery bag near the front door. "But I may have a future as an opera buff yet. My father may have brainwashed me a bit, disappointment tends to rub off, but my main complaint has always been that operas aren't in English."

"English ones are," she commented.

"But not the great operas. Or, the ones you people call great ones. If they'd translate the damn things, they'd have a lot more patrons than they do now."

"Translate them?" Margot laughed as she placed her handful of plastic in the bag. "I suppose you like colorized movies, too."

"It's not the same thing. Besides, they translate movies for foreign audiences."

"Sure, but that's movies."

"I sense a bit of cultural condescension in your tone."

"Well, it is a bit insulting to suggest translating operas."

"Sure, to the Italians it is." Bellamy laughed and sat on her couch. "Oh, this couch is a bit stiff. We'll have to figure out a way to break it in."

"Gee, I wonder what we might do?" Margot joined him, enjoying the feeling of sitting on her own couch in her own home for the first time in her life. "Opera wouldn't be the same in translation, you know," she told him. "The English words wouldn't fit the music."

"I know, but you can see my point."

"It sounds like we need more people writing English operas," she said, nestling comfortably into the crook of his arm. "Are you volunteering?"

"No way could I deal with musicians on a regular basis," he said. "I'll stick to novels."

"And I'll try to only take parts in English operas so you won't be too bored coming to hear me sing."

"No matter what language, it will never bore me to hear you sing," he said fervently.

"Well, in that case, I think we'll get along just fine."

"Famously," he agreed. "But not if we don't eat. Shall we go back to my place or are you stocked here?"

"If you like TV dinners, we could eat here. I don't have much else, besides fruit and vegetables."

"I've always been partial to meat in my meals," he said. "And the stuff in TV dinners doesn't qualify."

"Then it's your place. Come on, we can come back and hang pictures later."

"Boy, you're certainly in a hurry," he commented as they stood. "Expecting company?"

"No, it's just that...well, I guess I'm just excited. This is my first house, you know. It's thrilling."

"I know what you mean. When we first moved in, we..." But his words trailed off, leaving him looking perplexed for a moment. "Well, let's just say that I know what you mean."

"Yes, I know." Margot embraced him tightly, hoping to allow him a chance to fill in the spaces that occurred when he spoke of his late wife. It would take time, but time was one thing they had in abundance.

IT WAS NEARLY DARK when they sat down to a light meal in Bellamy's large kitchen. The last rays of the setting sun were glowing orange behind the roiling clouds over the calm Pacific, giving the horizon a look of heat and disquiet. A thin layer of fog was beginning to form along the ground, its ghostly tendrils moving up amid the bushes and the low stone wall encompassing Bellamy's patio.

"Here's to your newfound love of opera," Margot toasted, raising her glass of wine impishly. "And to your eventual acceptance of foreign tongues."

"Yeah, whatever," he replied, smiling, as he touched his glass to hers.

Watching Margot over his glass as he drank, Bellamy was suddenly aware of just how important she had become to him. He hadn't had time to think of such things when he'd rushed to her aid earlier but had merely acted on impulse. But now, seeing her again in such familiar surroundings, he was acutely aware of what the loss of her would mean. He couldn't remember ever considering such a thing with Kay, not at first, but the thought was inescapable now.

And yet, painful as it was to even briefly contemplate losing Margot, he felt warm knowing that he needed her so badly when he hadn't expected to need anyone like that again. He felt human again.

"What are you thinking about?" Margot asked. Though she knew he was a man prone to silences, the look of concentration on his face confused her.

"I was thinking that I don't ever want to lose you," he said.

"The odds are good that you won't."

"I want better than good."

"Okay, they're excellent." Margot reached out to touch his arm lightly, her heart seeming to swell at the touch of him. "At least, from this end they look excellent."

"But, Margot, I—" He stopped, wanting to bite the tongue that tried to speak these words, yet knowing that he should say it and be done. "Margot, I was just thinking that I wouldn't be able to stand losing you. But I was thinking about death, you know, accidents or such. I wasn't considering willing separation. And if you ever do want to be rid of me, please remind me to be a man about it. I really do love you enough to let you go if it comes to that. I just may need reminding."

"I won't have to remind you," she said. "Because I'll never grow tired of you. You can't see yourself, Bellamy, so you can't see what I see. I love you, and I will never stop loving you."

"Thank you," he said. Then he cleared his throat abruptly, blinking. "I've never been good at emotional scenes."

"So let's not have one. Come on, let's go play some Cole Porter." She stood with her glass and then took the bottle from the table as well. "I'll bring the wine."

"You'll be performing, won't you?" He joined her, slipping his arm around her shoulder as they walked to the hall and up the curving staircase.

"Certainly, it will be my first rehearsal with my own private accompanist."

"The first of many."

The telephone rang before they reached the piano, and Bellamy started toward it. Then he stopped, turning toward her.

"We don't need to take calls, do we?"

Margot sighed. "They'll probably only call back, anyway."

The telephone kept ringing, each explosion of sound seeming to grow louder and more insistent.

"Damn," he said, walking the rest of the way to the bedside receiver and picking it up. "Hello?"

Margot walked to the piano and sat, finishing her wine while he held a brief conversation and then hung up to return to her.

"Victor woke up," he said. "He asked for me."

"You should go see him," Margot said. "If he's asking for you in his condition, it's probably important that you go."

"I'll hurry."

"No, you won't." She bounced up from the bench and slipped her arms around him. "You'll obey the speed limit and drive carefully, won't you?"

"Yes, I will." He kissed her lightly, then passionately claimed her lips. "Yes, I will definitely drive safely."

"You're not feeling tight are you? I've got a bit of a buzz from the wine, myself."

"No, I'm okay. Body mass, you know."

"All right, then, I'll be here waiting for you."

"Keep the alarms on and don't open the door for anyone."

"Don't worry, I'm not going anywhere or doing anything unless it's with you. I'll just warm the bed for us."

"Good. We'll hang pictures tomorrow. Why don't you just start warming the bed right now? There's a television in that cabinet by the closet, if you'd like to burn off a few brain cells. I won't be more than a couple hours."

"Don't worry. Our opera phantom is in town now."

"I'll set the security before I go so that even a broken window will bring a cop running."

"Very good. And, Bellamy, if I'm asleep when you get back, wake me up this time." Margot rose up on her toes to plant a kiss on his lips, letting her hand drift down his body. "I definitely want to be awake the next time you get into bed with me."

"So do I," Bellamy said, nearly deciding against the trip right then and there. "Definitely."

Moments later, he was in his car driving cautiously through the thickening fog that had gathered around their homes. It grew progressively denser as he wound along the twisting highway, causing him to curse quietly about the weather that would surely make his return trip far longer than he would want. Tonight was not a good night to drive slowly.

MARGOT FINISHED his book over the next hour and then mounted the stairs to wait for her lover in the bedroom. The anticipation of his return was so intense that she knew she wouldn't be sleeping when he arrived.

The telephone rang as she got to the bedroom. She paused, looking at the instrument for a moment, and then lifted the receiver and answered it.

"Hello, love, I'm on my way back." It was Bellamy, although the static of the bad connection seemed to raise the pitch of his voice somewhat.

"That was fast."

"Yes, well, I've thought of something that could break this entire thing open for us," he said. "Meet me at your place. Okay?"

"Why?"

"I can't get into it," he said. "I hate driving and talking on this damn phone at the same time."

"Oh, that's why you sound so strange," she commented. "I didn't even notice the cellular phone in your car."

"Got to keep in touch, you know." Static consumed the line for a moment and then cleared away for her to hear him saying, "And I'll be there in ten minutes."

"Okay, I'll walk over now."

"Good. Bye-bye."

Wondering what it was that had Bellamy so excited, Margot turned off the security system in his big house and walked out alone into the mist.

THE AIR WAS COOL and damp, giving Margot a tingly feeling as she walked along the short stretch of road between Bellamy's house and hers. The mist was thick enough to totally obscure her unlit house in the moonless darkness, and she navigated entirely by the sight of a few yards of road ahead of her and watched for the turn to her home to come up on her right.

In the mist, the sounds of the ocean seemed miles away while the crunching sounds of her feet on the gravel shoulder of the road were amplified. Above her she could see nothing; the cloud cover was too thick to allow any moonlight through. It was as if she were alone in a cloud just drifting through the sky. In fact, the small movement of the mist around her did have a slightly unbalancing effect, giving her the feeling that she was walking sideways.

After a short time, when she thought she might have passed her turn, the sound of her footsteps became annoyingly loud—a continuous crunching that seemed to block out everything else. She stepped off the shoulder onto the asphalt surface of the roadway itself, which changed the crunch of her step to a slight tap. That was better, though it seemed that the crunching continued in her mind for several steps before it ceased abruptly.

That was odd. Margot felt a thrill of nervousness at the unexplained sound. She waited for a moment, twisting slightly in an attempt to look around her. She could see nothing but the dark gray of the softly swirling mist. There was nothing there.

This was foolishness. She had to get in out of the cold air or risk a sore throat. She began walking again, and just as expected, the turn to her home was only a couple of yards farther along the road.

As she turned toward home, however, another sound came through the still air. Not footsteps this time, but a breathy sound—like a sigh—coming from behind her. It was definitely a human sound, but so slight that she may have imagined it. Must have imagined it.

She began walking again. The reassuring crunch of her own footsteps on her gravel lane overcame any other sounds that might wish to interrupt her precarious calm. She passed her mailbox, which was empty, and continued along the driveway, which she resolved to have paved at the first chance. She passed a large bush to her left, and found herself pondering her lack of knowledge about shrubbery as she walked. Anything to keep her mind occupied and off thoughts of strange sounds and horrifying possibilities.

It didn't work. She imagined that her footsteps were producing a distinctly uneven echo, never quite keeping exact pace with her. She was imagining it, wasn't she?

Don't be a fool. You're alone here, she thought, re-
solving to maintain her steady pace even though it seemed
that the driveway might never end.

And then she heard someone softly singing....

BELLAMY PARKED in the hospital lot and jogged to the
entrance feeling tense from the long, gray drive. He
shouldn't have left her alone, he thought now. Victor was
out of danger and could have waited. Or he should have
brought Margot with him. But it was too late for hind-
sight now. All he could do was to go up to see his old
mentor and begin the slow journey back home.

As he walked up, Sergeant Terry, still working on his
investigation late into the night, was just emerging from
Victor's room.

"What brought you out tonight?" the policeman asked
him.

"Victor was asking for me," Bellamy said. "Is he
awake?"

"He's been sedated all day. It looks like we're back to
square one," he commented. "We let Neil Roberts go."

"What about the drug test? Won't you hold him on
that?"

"No, we didn't find anything in his apartment. Failing
one test isn't enough evidence to hold him."

"Did Victor see the man who attacked him?"

"No. He said he heard someone singing on stage and
went to check it out. Got jumped from behind. Clubbed
him and cut him."

"So it wasn't a purposeful attack?"

"Doesn't sound like it. Can't say either way on Pamela
Laurie yet. Could be she surprised someone, too."

"No motive?"

"No. Some maniac doesn't like opera, maybe."

"I would rather you'd told me that you had a motive at least."

"Sorry." The man shrugged, frowning. "They completed the autopsy on the carpenter, though. He was dead at least twenty-four hours before he went off the cliff."

"What?"

"Yes, he was strangled and somebody threw him off later."

"So he wasn't involved?"

"No, just got in the way. Well, I'm about done here. Is Miss Wylde safe?"

"Yes, she's at my place."

"Good."

Bellamy opened the door to Victor's room and stepped inside. A maze of tubes and wires led down to the frail-looking man in the bed from the many monitors and I.V. bottles clustered around him. His breath came in rasping but steady bursts, his chest lurching on each one, and his eyes were half-closed. But he was alert enough to have heard Bellamy enter the room and turned his head toward the door, a smile struggling to his pale lips.

"Edward," he whispered.

"Cut yourself shaving, eh, Maestro?" Bellamy drew up a chair beside the bed and leaned close to him. "Better buy an electric."

"I was dreaming of Margot," the older man said. He sighed, catching his breath again. "Dreaming of her singing to me. Such a song."

"Yes, a beautiful song," Bellamy agreed.

"No, no," Victor insisted weakly. "I wasn't dreaming." His eyes fluttered shut briefly, then he threw them open again. "Wasn't dreaming. I heard her sing on the stage."

His eyes closed again, and he began snoring softly, but roused himself briefly to look up at Bellamy.

"I went to ask what was wrong." He yawned, eyes fluttering. "Wrong with her voice."

"Why?"

"Someone stole her voice, Edward," the older man said. "Stole her voice."

"What? What do you mean?" Bellamy spoke insistently but quietly, finally giving up. His friend was sleeping.

Bellamy stood and left the room, completely perplexed by Victor's final words. Singing on stage? Someone stole her voice? He'd apparently dreamed of her singing on stage, but why he felt compelled to tell him about the dream now was beyond him. Well, the poor guy was drugged, so Bellamy couldn't expect him to be coherent.

Sergeant Terry was at the nurses' station when he came out of the room.

"Did you say that Victor was sedated all day?" Bellamy asked.

"Yes, just now was the first time I had any chance to talk to him," the officer said. "Why?"

"He seemed pretty dazed, is all. Who called me to come here?"

"It wasn't me." Sergeant Terry turned toward the nurse on duty. "Did anyone call Mr. Bellamy to come in tonight?"

"I don't have any record of it," she said, consulting a pad on her desk.

"Somebody called me," Bellamy mused. Then he turned toward Terry again. "Could you call the sheriff's department and have them send someone around to my place and check up on Margot? This doesn't feel right."

"I could drive out there."

"They'd be faster, I think. I'm going right back out, myself, but I'd like someone there as soon as possible."

"Sure. I'll have them wait with her until you arrive."

Bellamy whispered a fervent prayer as he rushed to the elevator. He had to get back to Margot. He only hoped that the stalker hadn't gotten to her first.

Chapter Fourteen

"Night and day, you are the one..."

Margot froze in place, her heart stilled within her. It was a man's voice, a clear high tenor, and she wasn't imagining it.

Walk! she urged herself. *Walk slowly and carefully.* She was amazed that she was able to do it while the man continued singing with growing conviction of undying, obsessive love.

Slipping her hand into the pocket of her jeans, she drew out the house key and held it tightly in her fist as she continued, allowing herself to walk a bit faster now that her key was in hand. Then the house presented itself as a darker shadow in the darkness of the mist that enveloped her. Almost there!

The singing stopped. Margot hesitated for a moment, listening. Yes, footsteps! Running footsteps.

She ran, too, rushing toward the safety of her home.

A sound to her left and then a flash of movement just barely visible were all the warning she had before her hair, streaming behind her as she ran, was grasped and jerked back, toppling her painfully to the ground.

Silence.

Margot rolled to her hands and knees and waited. There was nothing.

Then the man sang again, his voice higher this time in a perfectly trained falsetto. This time it was opera that he sang, one of her arias from *The Masque of the Red Death.*

She propelled herself forward like a sprinter coming out of the blocks, but she'd gotten turned around and was no longer headed toward the dark shape of the house. She stopped, turning in fright to get her bearings. Her movement had stopped his song, too, leaving her waiting for another sound, another indication of his presence even as she strained to find which way to run to safety.

She could hear the ocean on her right. If she turned to put that sound at her left she would be headed roughly back to the house, so she turned and began walking as quietly as possible. She could barely see her outstretched hand now, so dense was the mist. There would be no letup for hours.

She thought she could see the house once more, and began walking more quickly.

Then the song began again, right in front of her. A gray flash of movement produced wind upon her face and was gone. Then there was a footstep to her right and something touched her ear.

Margot cried out in alarm, but swallowed the sound as quickly as possible. She ran again only to be tripped full on her face.

"Oh, did you fall down?" The man spoke with overly deliberate compassion from directly above her. "Here, grab this and I'll pull you up."

Something cold touched her cheek and she cringed, fighting to identify it in the darkness. It came close again, and she could see what it was. The stolen sword.

"I sharpened it," he said. "I was surprised to find how dull it was."

"What do you want?" Margot whispered, barely able to get the words out as she rose slowly in preparation for her final sprint to the door.

"Nothing," he said. "I've already got it."

"Please, leave me alone," she pleaded. "Please."

"Oh, don't worry about me. Once I've had my smoke break, I'm just fine." He sounded so much like Pamela Laurie that she might have been fooled if she didn't know the woman was dead. "You prima donnas are a big pain in the butt."

Margot ran, stumbling on her front step, which was only a few feet before her rather than the great distance she'd expected. She struck the door bodily, knocking the wind out of herself for a moment. In this moment of confusion, she expected him to attack, but he did nothing. It was as though he'd never been there.

She managed to get the key into the lock and open the door, and then she slammed and chained it behind her. She stood gasping in the darkness of her home. She almost switched on the lights, but realized that she had no curtains yet. She began walking toward the kitchen, where the phone was.

No more than three steps into the room she was tripped by a chair lying in her path and fell to the floor, totally disoriented. There shouldn't have been anything there but there was, a kitchen chair lying on its side in the dining area. He'd been inside her house and rearranged everything!

Margot was frantic. Every direction she turned provided further fright. Tears of fear and frustration began to flow down her cheeks as she crawled swiftly to the kitchen telephone.

If she could just call 911 and then hide, she might be safe. The nightmare might yet be over. Yes, she was at the kitchen door and inside now. She stood and snatched the receiver from the cradle, putting it to her ear.

There was no dial tone.

He was in the house with her!

BELLAMY HUNG UP the telephone and ran from the hospital cursing himself, the fog, the police, the killer and himself again. He reached his car out of breath and jammed himself behind the wheel. His car squealed out of the parking lot before he'd closed his door.

There had been no answer at his house. *I should have known better than to leave her alone for any reason!* His second call, to Margot's house, had been answered by a message that the phone was "out of service." *I should have stayed home! Should have taken her along!*

The light ahead turned red, trapping him behind three cars at the intersection, while Margot was in danger miles away. He felt impotent and foolish sitting there tapping his fingers on the steering wheel and waiting for the red to change to green. But the sidewalk was empty and there was no one parked at the curb...

Grinning, Bellamy twisted the wheel and accelerated over the curb, piloting his sports car along the sidewalk and twisting the wheel to slide into the startled flow of traffic crossing his way. Horns blared around him but they let him in, and he began maneuvering to gain headway in the stream of cars.

Margot had been right. Everyone had been injured in the throat. Anne, the drunken carpenter, Pamela and Victor—all throat wounds. But the killer had concealed the carpenter's connection, leaving it up to the evidence of an autopsy to make the connection clear.

*He must have killed that poor kid shortly after I fin-
ished talking to him,* Bellamy thought as he drove onto the
freeway. He'd killed him and hidden his pickup and then
brought the body back to blame for the frightening game
he'd played with Margot.

Anne had thought she heard Margot singing in her
dressing room; Margot thought her tormenter the other
night was a woman; Victor thought he had heard Margot
singing and was going to ask after the health of her voice.

Someone had stolen her voice! That had to mean
something, but what?

Bellamy roared along the freeway, leapfrogging the few
cars out in the fog and gaining as much time as he could.
The pavement was becoming slick from the mist, causing
him to skid as he turned off on the road south. He could
only hope that Deputy Simmons had gotten there already
and was guarding Margot, because he wasn't going to
make very good time in this weather.

The mist swelled in around his car when he left the
freeway, becoming a tunnel and then an all-encompassing
cloud as he drove, ever slower, up the incline toward
Margot.

"HELLO," he said. He sounded uncannily like Bellamy
then, and the sound sickened her. He switched on a
flashlight, directing the beam up against the Red Death
mask he wore over his face. The light glimmered on the
sword he held up at his side. He was dressed in black and
wearing the old-fashioned opera cape, complete with red
silk lining. "I took the liberty of disconnecting your
phone. We don't want to be disturbed." It was Victor
Grimaldi talking then.

"I'm going to make this quick," he said, as Daniel
Pressman now. His lips, visible below the harsh red form

of the devil's mask, twisted into a harsh smile. "Yes, very quick would be good. Wouldn't it?"

"Who the hell are you?" Margot demanded. But the knowledge broke through to her even as she asked him. He was the mimic, Martin Andrews. He was the company member they'd thrown out who went on to become so wealthy that he was above suspicion. "Martin Andrews?"

"A pleasure to meet you," he said, in a voice that was probably his own. "But then, I've had you for a couple days already. Now I've got to get rid of you."

"You've had what?" The kitchen door was behind her. If the chain was off, she could get through it quickly. His hands were full now.

"Well, I've had . . ." He paused, cocking his head. "A visitor, I think." The flashlight was turned off, and she heard his footsteps. "Don't go away."

The front door opened and closed just as car lights created a yellow glow in the fog outside the kitchen window. Then the lights went out and a car door slammed.

Margot ran to the dining room window and peered out but she could see nothing in the inky blackness outside. She turned on the living room light, stood to the side of the window and stared out. The light reached only far enough to allow her to make out the sheriff's insignia on the side of the car outside and the faint hump of the lights on the roof, but she couldn't see the driver or Andrews.

Then there was a gunshot, and Margot jumped back from the window. Had he gotten him? Was she safe now?

"Miss Wylde?" A deep voice called from outside the house.

"Are you all right!" Margot hurried to the front door and peered through the small window. She could see the officer's visored hat, but his head was turned away.

"Thank God, you came," she said as she threw the door open.

Deputy Sheriff Albert Simmons stood on the threshold for a moment, his eyes rolled back in his head and his mouth hanging slackly open. Then he fell to the floor with a sickening thump, the long blade of the sword standing straight up from between his shoulders.

BELLAMY HURLED his car into his driveway and raced to his house. Leaping from his automobile, he ran to the front door, found the key on his ring and used it, running into the house calling Margot's name. He expected to find her asleep in the bedroom, but even as he mounted the stairs, his heart told him not to trust his expectations.

The bed was empty. She wasn't in the house!

He nearly fell in his headlong descent down the broad curving stairs and rushed blindly back through the house and to his car.

She had better be all right or someone is going to be very sorry, he thought as he threw the car into gear. But they wouldn't be sorry for long, because he didn't expect that anyone who harmed Margot would have very long to live with their regrets.

The fog was worse here than it had been on the drive up the cliff, but he floored the accelerator in the driveway and took full advantage of the sports car's steering capabilities to manage the turn south onto the roadway. He missed Margot's driveway, and bounced through the low ditch along the road and onto her property, hitting the brakes just in time to avoid slamming into a row of bushes along her sidewalk.

The deputy's car was parked by the house. Beyond it Bellamy could see a yellow glow in the mist and he sprinted toward it.

Deputy Simmons was lying across the threshold in a pool of blood. Bellamy knelt over the body, examining the ragged gash of a thrusting wound in the back of the deputy's uniform jacket.

The sword! Bellamy thought. *The bastard's got the sword!*

A footstep sounded, and Bellamy jumped back from the door just as a form came out of the fog at him. Steel moved in a gleaming arc that missed his head by inches. The figure retreated, falling back into the fog, and Bellamy pursued him without thinking. Margot's safety was the only thing in his mind.

The hiss of the blade passing through the air alerted him of the danger this time, but Bellamy managed to duck away from the assault. He spun around, straining to see, but only caught the briefest of glimpses as the dark form came at him in the fog.

The sword struck Bellamy just above the hip with a hot burst of pain. Bellamy instinctively grabbed the blade of the weapon and twisted it away from his attacker. Then he fell to one knee in the darkness, pain overcoming all other sensations as he struggled to hold the hilt of the sword in his bleeding hands.

Deprived of his weapon, perhaps satisfied that Bellamy was defeated, the man in the mist had gone.

He's gone after Margot! But Bellamy only managed to rise halfway to his feet before he fell half-conscious to the ground.

MARGOT'S ATTACKER began to laugh, his voice coming from somewhere in the deadly mist. After finding the deputy's body, she'd run outside realizing that there was no safety in the house.

The tower! If she could lock herself in the light tower, she might be safe until Bellamy arrived.

But no, if he found his house empty, he would come here only to meet Martin Andrews in the mist outside. She had to be able to warn him. But she could warn him! All she had to do was get into the tower!

She reached the tower door, threw it open and leaped into the darkness beyond. She secured the lock, thanking God that there was a lock on the door at all, and leaned breathlessly against the door.

Okay, take it easy. Your house keys are in your pocket, so he can't get in here from either door. You're safe now.

But it would only be a matter of minutes before he thought to break a window, so Margot began fumbling toward the staircase that ran up the wall of the tower. She stumbled against the stack of boxes near the base of the stairs, nearly falling before catching her balance against the wall and feeling her way along it until she found the first step. She didn't dare turn on a light for fear it would help him more than her, but climbed carefully up through the darkness.

Margot wasn't even halfway up the stairs when a sudden blast, like a large firecracker going off in the house, froze her in her steps. A gunshot! At first she thought that help might have arrived, but realized with mounting horror that Andrews had gotten the deputy's gun and was shooting the lock on the door. She began climbing faster as several more shots rang out, six in all, and then a spear of light shot into the tower below her.

"Rapunzel, Rapunzel, let down your hair!" he called out to her in a mockery of Bellamy's voice. Then the tower was flooded with light as he flipped the switch by the door. "You should buy a Stairmaster for exercise. It's much easier than this," he said, laughing.

Margot didn't dare look down, but she could hear his movements ringing on the iron steps as he climbed after her. She reached the top and climbed into the tower room, which was awash with moonlight bursting through a gap in the clouds overhead. Above the fog, the world was an ethereal place, with clouds both above and below her.

She moved away from the trapdoor quickly, circling toward the steel box with the large switch that would power the fog light. She reached it just as the dark form of his head rose above the trap. Praying that the light would work at all, Margot threw the switch.

There was a loud click, and then the huge lamp flickered and came to life, filling the tower room with a hellish light as its ancient mechanism began turning with a squealing groan.

"You couldn't stay out of the spotlight, could you?" he asked, laughing. "Or are you worried about ships at sea?"

The light swept across him, and he staggered back, throwing his hand up before his masked face in a futile attempt to protect his eyes from the harsh beam. Margot used the opportunity to get the light between them, turning her head away when it swept over her.

"What do you want?" she asked him. "Why are you doing this to me?"

"I want your voice, of course," he said, blinking the sight back into his burned retinas. He turned away from the light, though Margot knew that it was still uncomfortably bright. "And I have it, as you've heard, so why should you stick around?"

"That's crazy."

"Yeah, that's what my shrink told me," he said. He slammed the trapdoor shut and began circling the light toward her. "I had to rid the world of him, too. His was a boring voice, though, so I didn't keep it. There are too many psychiatrists in the world anyway. Don't you agree?''

"No, apparently there aren't," she said. Now that she could see him, she felt safer, and she kept moving to maintain her position with the rotating hump of the light between them.

"You people are so smug, aren't you? Not so smug now, though. None of you are in the end."

"Is that why you've been killing people? Because they're smug? You might consider suicide next, in that case."

"You're so funny. I'm in no mood to laugh, though. I'm quite winded from my climb." He was smiling as he spoke, and held the opera cape shut before him theatrically.

"They seemed to think that they could get along without me," he said. "I've showed them that they can't. While I, on the other hand, have gone on to fame and fortune without them. I never needed Victor's approval to make my way, did I? I never needed Pamela's constant carping. I don't need any of them."

"You must have needed something," she said as she passed the door to the balcony and continued mirroring his movement on the other side of the sweeping light. "Otherwise, why bother with all of this? If they weren't important, you wouldn't have wasted your time on them."

"I did need something," he admitted. He threw the cape back over his shoulders with a flair, showing the gun in his right hand. "I needed to have the best. I needed to be the best. Now that I've got your voice in my collection, I can move on. I have a flight booked to Italy for tomorrow."

"They were right about you," she said. She had to keep him bragging long enough for Bellamy to arrive and find them. "You are a self-important bum."

"Of course I'm self-important," he said, laughing as he ducked the turning light. The lamp was so bright that it obliterated even the black color of his cape with its glare. "I have every reason to be."

"You're insane."

"A marginal point, I assure you." He kept smiling as he spoke, a diabolical smile that didn't reach the dead centers of his eyes staring out of the mask. "Gave you quite a scare with the rail gag, didn't I? It's too bad that scribbler was there to stop your fall."

"He'll be here to stop this one, too," she said. The light had heated the small room, and sweat began to break out on her forehead. She brushed the moisture away with the back of her hand.

"He's been and gone," Andrews told her. "I dispatched that idiot with my trusty sword."

Margot's blood froze in her veins and she stood rooted in place as the light moved over her, so bright that it took her breath away and left her shaking against the cold window at her back. Bellamy dead? No, it couldn't be. He couldn't have! But he could have, and her own life suddenly held little value to her. When her heart began pumping again, it did so with a ragged pain in her chest.

"Where's your sword now?" she whispered, unable to find her voice.

"Your boyfriend put up a fight. Probably cut off all of his fingers when he grabbed it." Andrews laughed, walking more quickly toward her now. "I'll find it when I'm done here. A sword is such a noble weapon, and now that I've gone to the trouble of sharpening it, I'd like to use it again."

"You're totally crazy," she told him. "Your doctor should have put you down like a rabid dog instead of trying to treat you."

"We're all entitled to our opinions," he said.

Now she knew what she would do. Without Bellamy, there was no rescue and no life for which to be rescued. But, if she was going to die, she would take this madman with her. She resolved to send them both flying to the rocks below if she had the chance. She stopped walking when she reached the door to the balcony and stood with her hand on the knob, waiting for him to come around to her.

"Shall we sing together?" He approached her casually, his grin broadening when he saw that she'd given up trying to get away from him. "A lovely duet, perhaps? I never have the chance to sing a duet with my voices."

"You sing for me," she told him. "I want to hear you."

He walked over the trapdoor, coming to her side as he began to sing. The words seemed to drop in the overheated air, losing their momentum the moment they left his lips.

"Open the door," he said. "This room is too dead."

"Nothing will help your singing," she told him.

"Don't you say that!" He slapped her, knocking her to her knees. "Don't!" The butt of the revolver crashed down on her back, dropping her to her face on the floor, where she lay blinking in pain.

She lay gasping for a moment, staring at the toes of his running shoes as the blinding pain in her back slowly ebbed. That was when she saw the trapdoor move slightly, rising up from the floor with agonizing slowness!

He lied about Bellamy! she thought. With renewed energy, she pushed herself up. "Okay, I'm sorry. Please, I would like to hear you properly."

"Better," he said. "Now, open the door and step out."

She did as she was told, trying to keep her eyes off the trapdoor as she fought with the rusty knob.

Finally it turned as she pushed the door open.

He came through behind her, singing, and stood with his back against the glass wall of the tower room, well back from the missing section of railing. His voice was nearly able to reach the same heights as hers, clearly a well-trained instrument. But it was as false as the mask he wore over his face. There was no joy in his voice, no emotion, only a nearly perfect mimicry like that of a trained bird, and he continued looking at her with blank birdlike eyes as he sang.

Behind him, the door rose and Bellamy laid it carefully back, leaning for a moment against it as though tired from the climb. Margot watched past the singer's dark form as Bellamy brought the long sword up and used it as a cane to walk the rest of the way up the tower steps.

Then Bellamy turned toward the glass, and Margot saw the blood saturating his clothing at his side, and the blood running down the sword from where he held it. She gasped instinctively, her eyes widening.

"What?" Andrews stopped singing. He turned, staring at the author who was moving haltingly toward the open door. "Oh, bother," he said. He raised the gun and stepped into the doorway to meet Bellamy.

"No!" Margot screamed in fear and jumped at him. He shoved her back, and she staggered and fell to the balcony deck. Then he turned back and trained the gun on Bellamy's chest.

"Goodbye," he said, squeezing the trigger.

The hammer clicked down on an empty cylinder.

"Goodbye," Bellamy said, gasping for breath. He lifted the sword before him like a lance and charged as the light caught them in its merciless beam.

Blinded, Martin Andrews threw the empty gun as he tried to step out of Bellamy's path. The sword struck him, and Bellamy rushed into him, pushing him back where there should have been a railing.

But there was no railing, and Martin Andrews flew back, flailing frantically to find something solid between him and the rocks hidden below. His cape caught the ragged end of the broken railing, snagging and holding him for a tantalizing moment. But the fabric gave way and he fell into the mist.

He was gone, leaving only the sound of his screaming voice behind him. After a brief echo, that, too, was gone.

"I think you'd better put an elevator in this thing," Bellamy said then. He fell back against the window, slowly sliding along the glass until he was seated on the deck. "That was a long climb."

"My God, Bellamy, are you all right?" Margot rushed to his side, throwing her arms around him and kissing his face with relief. "No, of course you're not all right. We've got to get you downstairs. Can you make it?"

"Oh, sure," he said, trying to laugh as he smiled at her. "Down is easy from here."

"Too easy," she agreed. "But I think we'll take the stairs if you don't mind. The express route ends rather abruptly."

Bellamy managed a smile. "Well, now that you're safe, the opera should be a success, at any rate."

"Only because we have the best writer," she said, smiling back.

He chuckled. "One who now has the beginning for a plot to his next horror novel."

"What?" she asked, her smile broadening.

"Oh, you know," he replied. "Beautiful opera diva under a grave threat . . ."

Her brows suddenly narrowed. "I hope Anne and Victor are okay."

"They'll be fine," he reassured her.

The clouds overhead were clearing, sending the glorious light of the moon down on the lighthouse and fog-shrouded sea as they began their descent down the stairs.

"Oh," Bellamy said, drawing her close and kissing her ear. "There's one other thing."

"Getting you to a doctor?"

"No." Bellamy managed another smile. "Can I move into your lighthouse?"

"Yes," Margot whispered, glad the possibility for a permanent position was open to her. "Oh, yes."

...And here's more of the best in romantic suspense!

Turn the page for a bonus look at what's in store for you next month, in Harlequin Intrigue #253 WHAT CHILD IS THIS?—a special Christmas edition in Rebecca York's 43 Light Street series.

In the hallowed halls of this charming building, danger has been averted and romance has blossomed. Now Christmas comes to 43 Light Street—and in its stocking is all the action, suspense and romance that your heart can hold.

Chapter One

Guilty until proven innocent.

Erin Morgan squinted into the fog that turned the buildings on either side of Light Street into a canyon of dimly realized apparitions.

"Guilty until proven innocent," she repeated aloud.

It wasn't supposed to work that way. Yet that was how Erin had felt since the Graveyard Murders had rocked Baltimore. Ever since the killer had tricked her into framing her friend Sabrina Barkley.

Sabrina had forgiven her. But she hadn't forgiven herself, and she was never going to let something like that happen again.

She glanced at the purse beside her on the passenger seat and felt her stomach knot. It was stuffed with five thousand dollars in contributions for Santa's Toy and Clothing Fund. Most were checks, but she was carrying more than eight hundred dollars in cash. And she wasn't going to keep it in her possession a moment longer than necessary.

Erin pressed her foot down on the accelerator and then eased up again as a dense patch of white swallowed up the car. She couldn't even see the Christmas decorations she knew were festooned from many of the downtown office windows.

"'Tis the season to be jolly..." She sang a few lines of the carol to cheer herself up, but her voice trailed off in the gloom.

Forty-three Light Street glided into view through the mist like a huge underwater rock formation.

Erin drove around to the back of the building where she could get in and out as quickly as possible. Pulling the collar of her coat closed against the icy wind, she hurried toward the back door—the key ready in her hand.

It felt good to get out of the cold. But there was nothing welcoming about the dank, dimly lit back entrance—so different from the fading grandeur of the marble foyer. Here there were no pretensions of gentility, only institutional gray walls and a bare concrete floor.

Clutching her purse more tightly, she strained her ears and peered into the darkness. She heard nothing but the familiar sound of the steam pipes rattling. And she saw nothing moving in the shadows. Still, the fine hairs on the back of her neck stirred as she bolted into the service elevator and pressed the button.

Upstairs the paint was brighter, and the tile floors were polished. But at this time of night, only a few dim lights held back the shadows, and the clicking of her high heels echoed back at her like water dripping in an underground cavern.

Feeling strangely exposed in the darkness, Erin kept her eyes focused on the glass panel of her office door. She was almost running by the time she reached it.

Her hand closed around the knob. It was solid and reassuring against her moist palm, and she felt some of the knots in her stomach untie themselves. With a sigh of relief, she kicked the door closed behind her, shutting out the unseen phantoms of the hall.

Reaching over one of the mismatched couches donated by a local rental company, she flipped the light switch. Nothing happened. Darn. The bulb must be out.

In the darkness, she took a few steps toward the file room and stopped.

Something else was wrong. Maybe it was the smell. Not the clean pine scent of the little Christmas tree she'd set up by the window, but the dank odor of sweat.

She was backing quietly toward the door when fingers as hard and lean as a handcuff shot out and closed around her wrist.

A scream of terror rose in her throat. The sound was choked off by a rubber glove against her lips.

Someone was in her office. In the dark.

Her mind registered no more than that. But her body was already struggling—trying to twist away.

"No. Please." Even as she pleaded, she knew she was wasting her breath.

He was strong. And ruthless.

Her free hand came up to pummel his shoulder and neck. He grunted and shook her so hard that her vision blurred. She tried to work her teeth against the rubbery palm that covered her mouth.

His grip adroitly shifted to her throat. He began to squeeze, and she felt the breath turn to stone in her lungs.

He bent her backward over his arm, and she stared up into a face covered by a ski mask, the features a strange parody of something human.

The dark circles around the eyes, the small red circle around the mouth, the two dots of color on his cheeks wavered in her vision like coins in the bottom of a fountain.

The pressure increased. Her lungs were going to explode.

No. Please. Let me go home. I have a little boy. He needs me.

The words were choked off like her life breath.

Like the rapidly fading light. She was dying. And the scenes of her life flashed before her eyes. Climbing into bed with her parents on Sunday morning. First grade. High school graduation. Her marriage to Bruce. Kenny's birth. Her husband's death. Betraying Sabrina. Finishing college. Her new job with Silver Miracle Charities. The holiday fund-raiser tonight.

The events of her life trickled through her mind like the last grains of sand rolling down the sloping sides of an hourglass. Then there was only blackness.

Don't miss this next 43 Light Street tale—#253 WHACHILD IS THIS?—*coming December 1993—only from Rebecca York and Harlequin Intrigue!*

HARLEQUIN®
INTRIGUE®

'Tis the season...

**for a special Christmas ''43 Light Street'' book
from Rebecca York!**

43
Light St.

All wrapped up, especially for you, is Rebecca York's gift
this Christmas—a heartwarming tale of suspense and
holiday emotion.

What Child is This?

Two people, drawn together by circumstance and bound
together by love, put their hearts and lives on the line to
uncover the secret of the *real* meaning of Christmas....

In December, don't miss # 253 WHAT CHILD IS THIS?—coming
to you just in time for Christmas, only from
Harlequin Intrigue.

Take 4 bestselling love stories FREE

Plus get a FREE surprise gift!

Special Limited-time Offer

Mail to Harlequin Reader Service®

3010 Walden Avenue
P.O. Box 1867
Buffalo, N.Y. 14269-1867

YES! Please send me 4 free Harlequin Intrigue® novels and my free surprise gift. Then send me 4 brand-new novels every month. Bill me at the low price of $2.24 each plus 25¢ delivery and applicable sales tax, if any.* That's the complete price and—compared to the cover prices of $2.99 each—quite a bargain! I understand that accepting the books and gift places me under no obligation ever to buy any books. I can always return a shipment and cancel at any time. Even if I never buy another book from Harlequin, the 4 free books and the surprise gift are mine to keep forever.

181 BPA AJJE

Name	(PLEASE PRINT)
Address	Apt. No.
City	State	Zip

This offer is limited to one order per household and not valid to present Harlequin Intrigue® subscribers.
*Terms and prices are subject to change without notice. Sales tax applicable in N.Y.

UINT-93R   ©1990 Harlequin Enterprises Limited

HARLEQUIN®

I N T R I G U E®

CHRISTMAS STALKINGS

All wrapped up in
spine-tingling packages,
here are two books
sure to keep you on
edge this holiday season!

#254 SANTA CLAUS IS COMING
by M.J. Rodgers

On the first day of Christmas, newscaster Belle Breeze was
sung a bad rendition of "The Twelve Days of Christmas."
Then, one by one, the gifts started to arrive, and Belle knew
the twelfth gift would play havoc with her very life....

#255 SCARLET SEASON
by Laura Gordon

The night was *too* silent when, on a snowy Denver street,
Cassie Craig found herself the lone witness to a crime that no
one believed happened. Her search for the truth would make
this Christmas season chilling....

DON'T MISS THESE SPECIAL HOLIDAY INTRIGUES
IN DECEMBER 1993!

HIX

Curl Up With Someone Familiar

Familiar is back! The fantastic feline with a flair for solving crimes makes his third Harlequin Intrigue appearance in:

#256   THRICE FAMILIAR
by Caroline Burnes
December 1993

When a valuable racehorse is stolen from a horse farm in Scotland, it's Familiar's first chance to gain international acclaim. And it's the perfect opportunity for him to practice his pussyfooting panache, as he tries to matchmake the horse's owner and trainer, Catherine Shaw and Patrick Nelson—two people as opposite as cats and dogs!

Don't miss #256 THRICE FAMILIAR—for *cat*-astrophic intrigue and *purr*-fect romance!

FEAR-F

HARLEQUIN®

I N T R I G U E®

WHO ARE THESE

Women of Mystery

They say what makes a woman alluring is her air of mystery.
Next month Harlequin Intrigue brings you two *very* mysterious women—Erika Rand and Judi Lind.
We're proud to introduce these two authors new to Harlequin Intrigue.

And not only are the authors "Women of Mystery"—
so are the heroines!

Catherine Monroe is hiding—in the heart of the
Amazon…behind a veil of mystery.…
Anne Farraday is hiding—in someone else's life…
behind someone else's name.…
When they meet the right man, their lips may tell tales, but
their eyes can't mask desire.….

**Don't miss
#259 LYING EYES by Erika Rand
#260 WITHOUT A PAST by Judi Lind
January 1994**

**Be on the lookout for more "Women of Mystery" in the
months to come, as we search out the best new writers, just
for you—only from Harlequin Intrigue!**   WOMEN

1993 Keepsake

CHRISTMAS

Stories

Capture the spirit and romance of Christmas with KEEPSAKE CHRISTMAS STORIES, a collection of three stories by favorite historical authors. The perfect Christmas gift!

Don't miss these heartwarming stories, available in November wherever Harlequin books are sold:

ONCE UPON A CHRISTMAS by Curtiss Ann Matlock
A FAIRYTALE SEASON by Marianne Willman
TIDINGS OF JOY by Victoria Pade

ADD A TOUCH OF ROMANCE TO YOUR HOLIDAY SEASON WITH KEEPSAKE CHRISTMAS STORIES!

HX93

Harlequin is proud to present our
best authors and their best books.
Always the best for your
reading pleasure!

Throughout 1993, Harlequin will bring you
exciting books by some of the top names in
contemporary romance!

In November, look for

BARBARA
DELINSKY

First, Best and Only

Their passion burned even stronger....

CEO Marni Lange didn't have time for nonsense like
photographs. The promotion department, however,
insisted she was the perfect cover model for the launch
of their new career-woman magazine. She couldn't
argue with her own department. She should have.

The photographer was a man she'd prayed never
to see again. Brian Webster had been her first—
and best—lover. This time, could she play
with fire without being burned?

Don't miss FIRST, BEST AND ONLY by Barbara Delinsky...
wherever Harlequin books are sold.

BOB6

When the only time you have for yourself is...

STOLEN *moments* ™

Christmas is such a busy time—with shopping, decorating, writing cards, trimming trees, wrapping gifts....

When you do have a few *stolen moments* to call your own, treat yourself to a brand-new *short* novel. Relax with one of our Stocking Stuffers—or with all six!

Each STOLEN MOMENTS title is a complete and original contemporary romance that's the perfect length for the busy woman of the nineties! Especially at Christmas...

And they make perfect **stocking stuffers,** too! (For your mother, grandmother, daughters, friends, co-workers, neighbors, aunts, cousins—all the other women in your life!)

Look for the STOLEN MOMENTS display in December

STOCKING STUFFERS:

HIS MISTRESS Carrie Alexander
DANIEL'S DECEPTION Marie DeWitt
SNOW ANGEL Isolde Evans
THE FAMILY MAN Danielle Kelly
THE LONE WOLF Ellen Rogers
MONTANA CHRISTMAS Lynn Russell

HSM2

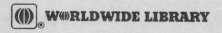

WORLDWIDE LIBRARY